A Sir Galahad
of Her Own

Joyce Armintrout

Copyright © 2014 Joyce Armintrout
All rights reserved
First Edition

PAGE PUBLISHING, INC.
New York, NY

First originally published by Page Publishing, Inc. 2014

ISBN 978-1-62838-859-6 (pbk)
ISBN 978-1-62838-860-2 (digital)

Printed in the United States of America

Chapter One

Wind tugged at her coat as the rain pelted her bowed head. Raindrops mingled with tears as they coursed down her cheeks. The slim dejected figure was unaware of the storm raging around her as she trudged along the edge of the narrow blacktop road.

She had traveled this road, to and from the Eastland factory, for the past year and a half.

The job had been her salvation because the money she earned had enabled her to pay for a sitter for the twins and the tuition for her night classes. Her schooling was important to her because she knew it would be difficult for her to be taken as a serious interior decorator unless she had the proper credentials to back it up.

Everything had changed now. She and about half of her coworkers had been laid off effective immediately.

Six months ago, the company's owner had been killed in a plane crash. His son, according to newspaper reports, had been seriously injured and faced months of convalescence. Another son had taken over the operation of the factory and as far as anyone knew, the business was operating normally. According to her foreman, there had been some sort of financial problem that had forced the severe cutback of jobs at this time.

What was she going to do? Luci was working regularly now, so maybe she could help out a little bit more. At least until Chris could figure out some way to make enough money to finish her night school classes. The twins had to be tended to, and she was afraid to trust Luci to come home and watch them on the nights that she attended her classes.

Just a few more weeks. That's all she needed.

She was so deep in her thoughts that she failed to hear the car approaching from behind. The sound of a car horn so startled her that she slipped on the wet road surface and pitched sideways into the ditch. That was the final straw! She wanted to just remain there and cry her eyes out, but almost immediately, strong arms were lifting her up. Before she realized what was happening, she felt herself being gently placed upon the softest leather car seat she had ever felt.

"Are you all right?" an anxious voice asked.

"What the devil are you doing out in this storm?" the same voice demanded.

Numbly, Chris raised her head to look into the face of the man who had almost run her down and then become her rescuer. She tried to speak, but no words would come. It was almost too much of an effort for her to keep her eyes open, let alone say anything, so she just allowed her head to fall against the back of the seat.

Quickly the stranger removed his coat to cover the rain-soaked girl. Gently he drew the garment across her trembling shoulders, closed the door quietly as though not to disturb her, and returned to his seat behind the steering wheel. He watched her for a few moments, waiting for her to say something.

"Are you all right?" he asked for a second time.

"You scared me half to death!" He continued after a moment, "I asked why you were out in this storm. You could have been killed! You should have had better sense!" He stopped talking and took a deep breath, trying to calm himself. He ran his fingers through his black curly hair wet from the rain and sat motionless for another moment watching the storm raging outside his windshield.

She jumped when his fist came crashing down on the steering wheel. "Don't just sit there!" His patience had run out. He wasn't used to being ignored, but more than that, he was starting to worry that the girl might really be hurt.

"Say something! Anything! Why were you walking in a storm like this?"

"I'm sorry," she mustered up the energy to make a faint reply. "I'm all right—just a little shaky. Please, I just want to go home because the twins will be there soon, and I need to be there for them."

"Where do you live?"

"It isn't very far, so I can walk. I do it all of the time." She tried in vain to find the door handle. "I've caused you too much trouble already."

"I said, where do you live?" he snapped. "I'm taking you home before anything else happens to you."

Too miserable to argue, Chris gave him instructions to her house, then sank back against the seat and closed her eyes.

She was unaware of the concerned green eyes that kept straying from the wet road to the frail-looking passenger, nor did she notice when the car came to a halt in front of her house. When she made no move to get out, he reached over and gently brushed the wet hair back so he could more clearly see her face.

"Please don't cry," he coaxed when he saw a single tear make it's was down her cheek.

"Everything will be all right. You will feel better once you get in the house and dried off. I'm sorry if I startled you. You might not have fallen if I hadn't distracted you."

He attempted to soothe her. He couldn't stand to see anyone cry, especially since he was most likely the cause of the tears.

"No, it was my fault. I should have been paying more attention," she protested. "Thank you for being so kind." She slipped the coat off her shoulders and pushed it aside as she once again searched for the door handle. Before she found it, the door opened, and strong arms lifted her out of the car. Her protests fell on deaf ears as he carried her up the walk. She noticed the rain had nearly stopped as he carefully set her down on the sidewalk near her front stoop.

"Can you stand?" he asked before he released his hold on her.

"Yes—I'm all right now. Well, thank you again for your help. I'll try to be more careful next time." Then she added, almost to herself, "Well, I guess there won't be a next time, so I won't need to worry about that."

"Why were you walking out there?" He couldn't let it go. He had to know.

"I was on my way home from the Eastland factory."

"Do you work there?"

"Up until a couple of hours ago, I did. This afternoon, about half of us got laid off."

"Do you know why you were let go?" a cautious voice asked.

"We heard there was some kind of financial problems. If they think they have money problems, they should get a load of what it will do to my finances," she added, wryly.

The stranger stood for a little bit, looking at the bedraggled young girl standing before him. He opened his mouth as if to say something, then apparently thought better of it and made no further comment. Yet he still stood, reluctant to walk away from her even though he had not the slightest idea the reason for his hesitation.

"Well, I'll go now. I'm sure when you are warmed up a bit and get into some dry clothes things will look a lot better."

Chris watched as he returned to his car. She noticed his stride was slightly irregular, not quite a limp, just not quite normal. As he got in the car, Chris remembered she hadn't asked his name. She guessed that it probably didn't matter because she doubted that she would ever see him again.

Then she remembered the twins and hurried up the steps to her front door. As was her custom, she used the key she kept around her neck to unlock the door. Her father had given it to her on her seventh birthday, and even to this day, she was seldom without it.

She quickly showered, donned fresh clothes, and hurried to the kitchen to begin fixing dinner.

While it was cooking, she gathered the laundry waiting to be done. She sorted the loads and started the first one, then returned to the kitchen to stir the pot simmering on the stove. She was so tired. Maybe Luci would help with some of the chores when she came home.

Luci was the older sister by two years, but it had fallen to Chris to run the house and keep the family, or what was left of it, together.

She sank down on a chair to rest a bit, her thoughts going back three years when her life had been carefree. Her parents were always there to see that the four children felt secure and happy. The house had always been full of love and laughter.

Then suddenly her world was shattered and their parents were gone!

Luci was just eighteen when it happened, Chris sixteen, and Jon and Jenny only three. Luci had been inconsolable. Chris was devastated, but there was no time for her to mourn as she tended the twins' needs. She tried to keep them busy during the day and held them tightly at night when they cried.

The sound of the school bus, as it came to a halt in front of the house, brought her out of her reverie. The twins were home.

She hurried to the door to greet them, as was her habit. As she opened it, Jon was rushing up the steps at top speed with Jenny following more sedately behind. The youngsters were almost identical in looks but near opposites in personality. Jon rarely saw a stranger, and Jenny preferred to cling to Chris when approached by someone she didn't know.

"I'm hungry. How soon can we eat?" Jon asked as he tried to duck past Chris in order to avoid the hug she had always given him. "Aw, Chris, I'm getting too big to be hugged!"

"Okay for now," Chris couldn't help but be amused at his evasive actions as she let the little boy go past her.

"We will eat as soon as it's ready. It shouldn't be long."

When Jenny reached the door, she hugged Chris tightly around her neck.

"How was your day, sweetie?"

"It was all right. I made a new friend today. Can I have her over to play sometime?"

"Of course you may. What is her name?"

"Her name is Sarah, and she's almost as old as I am. We played on the swings together at recess. She and her brother just moved here. They both are lonesome because they don't have any friends yet. I really like her, she's nice."

"We'll see about asking her over very soon. Now we had better get in the kitchen before your brother thinks he's going to starve to death."

Chris finished up the meal while the kids changed out of their school clothes and washed their hands. Tonight Chris had fixed them vegetable soup and tuna salad sandwiches. After they finished eating, she sent them out into the backyard to play a while. She stacked the dishes in the sink before she started another load of clothes in the washing machine. She was so tired, and that pain in her side was back. It was returning more often these days. She wished Luci would come home so she could help with the work. It would be nice to go to bed and rest until she felt better, but the work had to be done.

Sighing deeply, she sank into a chair once again to rest a moment before starting the dishes. She was still there when the doorbell roused her. It must be Luci.

"Did you forget your keys again?" she asked as she swung the door open.

"Oh, I'm sorry. I thought you were my sister," she stammered as she looked up into the same face she had bid good-bye to a couple of hours earlier.

"What are you doing here?"

"May I come in for a minute?" he asked.

"Of course. I'm so sorry. Please come in." She stepped back to make room for the broad-shouldered man to enter. As she turned back to face him, she noticed her purse dangling from his left hand.

"You look a little better than when last I saw you. You left this in my car, so I brought it by this evening because I thought you might be worried about its whereabouts." He grinned as he handed it to her.

"Actually, my mind has been on other things, and I hadn't missed it yet. Thank you for returning it to me, Mr.—I'm sorry, I don't even know your name." She waited for him to introduce himself.

"It's Phillip Cameron E—," he paused slightly, "everyone calls me Cam." After another brief pause, he added, "I'm afraid that I have a confession to make. I looked in your wallet and saw that your name is Christine Walker. That's a nice name. Is it Miss or Mrs.?"

"Please, call me Chris. And I'm afraid it's just plain Miss."

"If I may say so, you might well be a Miss, but you will never be *just plain*," he corrected her.

They stood awkwardly for a moment before the quiet of the house was shattered by the slamming of the back door and the sound of two sets of little footsteps coming across the kitchen floor.

"Who does that black car belong—?" Jon came to an abrupt halt when he spied Cam standing in the living room with his sister. Jenny followed Jon into the room, eyeing the strange man as she edged over to stand close beside Chris.

"Who are you?" Jon asked.

"My name is Cam," he answered as he dropped to one knee to talk to the curious boy.

They eyed each other for a moment before Chris remembered her manners and introduced the children to Cam.

"That's Jon you are eye to eye with, and this bashful young lady is Jenny. Children, this is Mr. Cameron."

"Please let them call me Cam. Anything else makes me feel like I'm over the hill."

Cam asked as he winked at Jon and solemnly extended his hand. Jon, equally serious, accepted the offered hand.

"Can we have a cookie?" Jon asked Chris. Apparently satisfied with Cam, he turned back to him and asked, "Would you like a cookie and some milk, too?"

"If your mother doesn't mind, I think that would be nice," he replied as he straightened up. Chris didn't fail to notice the effort it took him to return to his feet.

"She's not our mother, she's our sister." Jon giggled and even Jenny thought it was funny. As she grinned, Cam reached out his hand to her. After a small hesitation, Jenny slipped her small hand into his. She guessed if Jon thought he was safe, then he must be.

Cam looked at Chris but didn't move until she nodded approval, then he allowed Jenny to lead him to the kitchen.

"You don't have to drink milk. You may have coffee if you prefer." Chris smiled as she poured milk for the children and put a plate of homemade cookies on the table.

"That's the first time I've seen you smile. It becomes you," Cam observed.

"I would love a cup of coffee if you will have one also," he responded.

While she set about filling the coffee mugs, Cam surveyed the kitchen. The room had only one window and a door with the top half of glass. It would have been dark except for the sunny yellow-painted cabinets, soft cream countertops, white appliances, and sheer white valences over the window and door, allowing in extra light for the area. The round table at which they were seated, with its navy and white checked tablecloth, seemed to tie the whole room together and make it quite cheery.

"How come you came to see my sister?" The question surprised Chris because it came from Jenny. She rarely spoke to strangers, let alone asked them questions.

"I brought her home this afternoon, and she left something in my car. So I came back to return it to her."

"Are you going to come back again?" she asked.

"Jennifer! That's quite enough questions. Eat your cookie." Chris sought to stop any further inquiries.

She placed a mug in front of Cam and took a seat across from him with her coffee just as the phone rang. She excused herself and left the room to answer it.

"Hello."

"Hi, Sis, it's me. I have the most exciting news! It's a wonderful opportunity for me! There's a man from New York City here in the bar. We got to talking, and he knows people who can get me modeling jobs. He says he will help me get a job and supply everything I will need to get started. Isn't it great? The only thing is, he is on his way there now, and I have to go with him."

"Luci, you can't leave just like that! Why don't you come home and we'll discuss it. I lost my job today, and I don't know when I will find another."

"I'm sorry about your job, Sis, but I really have to do this. I'm going to need everything I have to get settled. I will try to send you some money as soon as I can."

"But, Luci, I really need you now. You have to watch the kids so I can finish my night classes. I'm almost finished, and it will be so much easier to find a job if I can get my degree first," she pleaded with Luci.

"I'm sorry, but I have to do this now because it may be the last chance I ever have to make something of myself. I know I can make it if only I have a chance. I need you to pack up my clothes and stuff, and I will call you when I get there to tell you where to send them."

"But Luci, you can't just take off like this with someone you don't even know! Besides, the children will want to say good-bye. Luci! Luci!" The phone went dead. Luci was gone.

She couldn't believe that even Luci would do something that stupid.

What was she going to do now without her sister? Chris asked herself.

Luci had always dreamed of becoming a professional model. All of her share of their parents' money had gone toward preparation for that. First there was modeling school, then charm school, and makeup classes. The last of her money had been used for a trip to New York City for job interviews. Nothing had come of that, so she had hoped Luci had given up her dreams and would settle down. She had been working as a waitress for a couple of months now, and Chris had been encouraging her to take some night classes to learn a skill.

Numbly, she replaced the receiver and returned to the kitchen. Her coffee was lukewarm, but she didn't notice as she took a sip. Her mind raced frantically trying to come up with a way to manage without Luci.

"We are finished, Chris. Can we take Cam out and show him our backyard?" Jon's voice broke into her chaotic thoughts.

Cam hadn't taken his eyes off of Chris since she had returned to the table. Before she could form an answer, he gently refused the children's offer.

"Maybe next time I come. Right now I need to talk to Chris."

Chris excused the children and absently reminded them to put on their jackets before they went outside.

After a moment, when Chris made no move, Cam voiced his concern.

"I'm sorry. I couldn't help but overhear your phone conversation. Who is Luci?"

"She is my sister," Chris answered quietly.

"Is she younger?"

"No, she is two years older."

"Where is she going?"

"New York City."

"Why is she going?"

"Please, I can't talk about it right now," she cut him off. "Would you like some more coffee?"

"No, thanks," he answered as she rose from her chair.

He sat for a time, watching the distraught girl before him as she moved around the room, pausing at the window looking out over the backyard. After a bit he got to his feet and moved to stand behind her, taking care not to touch her.

His eyes took in what hers were blind to for the moment. Two well-adjusted, happy children playing contentedly in a neatly manicured fenced yard. He didn't know much about the family yet, but his gut instinct told him that Chris had a great deal to do with what he had seen, both inside and outside the house.

He knew he was intruding, but his innate curiosity wouldn't let him leave without digging deeper into this family.

Where were the parents? Why was Luci leaving so suddenly? Chris seemed to be having real problems, and Cam wanted very much to help the family because he felt at least partially responsible for her troubles.

His instinct also told him that he was dealing with a very proud girl. One who had dealt with and conquered a great deal of adversity in her young life. He also knew that if he were going to be allowed to help, he was going to have to exercise diplomacy, tact, and all the subterfuge he could muster. But he was going to help her. He knew that for sure. There was something about her that tugged at his heart strings and would not have let him walk out of her life even if he were so inclined—which he wasn't.

"Do you or the children have any plans for tomorrow?" He had a glimmer of an idea. Maybe there was something he could do to at least keep her in his life for a little while longer.

"It's Saturday. Just the usual housework, laundry, and grocery shopping," she answered.

"I wonder if you would do me a big favor. Tomorrow is my niece's sixth birthday, and her grandmother is giving her a party. Her parents have just moved here, so she hasn't made any friends yet. She is really quite lonesome, so if you would let the twins attend the party, I'm sure it would make her very happy." He held his breath as he waited for her reaction.

Every instinct told her to refuse, but how could she deprive the children of a chance to have some fun? Heaven knows that didn't happen very often, and she knew they would enjoy the outing.

"I'm sure they would have a good time, but I don't think I can allow them to go to a stranger's house, especially since I don't have the faintest idea even where the grandmother lives."

She reluctantly refused the request.

"Of course you are invited also. I know that my sister would love to meet you, and I am equally sure you will like her. She's a fine person even if she is my sister. Please don't bring a gift. Sarah's grandmother spoils her rotten. She already has a mountain of stuff, and I understand she went shopping again today. Personally, I think they are going overboard because the child is lonesome. All she really needs is to find a friend. I'm hoping that will happen when she meets Jenny." Cam was struggling to come with a plausible explanation that she would believe as to why he was inviting them to the party.

"Really, Cam." Chris misunderstood his request. "I can afford to buy a gift for a little girl! I'm not that broke!"

"I'm sorry, I didn't mean to offend you," he apologized praying he hadn't blown it.

"You didn't. Just don't feel sorry for me. I hate being pitied!" she answered, somewhat mollified.

"I don't care if you bring a whole carload of stuff, as long as you and the kids come." Cam held his hands up in total surrender.

"Well, I guess it would be all right. Where is it going to be?" She took a deep breath, trying to mentally calculate how much a cab would cost and wondering if she would have enough money to pay for it.

"Don't worry about that. If it's acceptable, I will pick you all up at ten in the morning so the kids will have a chance to get to know each other before the party actually begins."

Cam sighed with relief and then added. "But right now, I have to go because I have an appointment that I must keep."

"Thank you for returning my purse and for inviting Jon and Jenny to the birthday party. I'm sure they will enjoy it," she said as she preceded him to the front door.

"It was no trouble at all," Cam brushed away her thanks. "On the contrary, thank you for allowing the kids to help make a lonely little girl happy on her birthday."

He hesitated for a moment, started to say something more, then thought better of it. He looked at her for another moment, then turned and left without further comment.

She stood watching his car until it disappeared from sight before closing the door. Just then the back door opened then slammed shut again as Jon came rushing into the room carrying a frog.

"Where's Cam?" he asked. "I want to show him Hoppy."

"He's gone, but you can tell him about it the next time you see him."

"Is he coming back?" the disappointed little boy asked hopefully.

"Not tonight, but I think he will tomorrow."

"How come?" Jon brightened at the prospect of seeing his new friend again.

"You and Jenny have been invited to a birthday party. He is going to pick us all up in the morning and take us there."

"Wow! A birthday party! With cake and presents and everything?"

"Yes, but this time you don't get the presents. You give them because the party is for someone else. But I'll bet that you will get cake and ice cream." Chris laughed as she bent to hug the little boy, being very careful not to touch the frog.

"Boy, wait 'til I tell Jen. I'll bet she will be surprised." He ducked away from Chris's attempted hug and hurried back outside to give Jenny the news.

Chris returned to the laundry. She had to get it done tonight because they would, in all probability, be gone most of the day tomorrow.

Time to remove another load from the dryer, refill it, and put another load in the washing machine. She washed the dishes and cleaned the kitchen while that load was drying. Her side was really beginning to ache now, but there were still things that had to be done.

She called the children in for their baths as soon as she finished the kitchen work.

They were so excited about the next day that she had to repeatedly urge them to finish their baths and get into their pajamas.

"If you two don't get into your beds right now, I'm going to call Cam and tell him that you won't be able to go tomorrow because you stayed up too late tonight and you will be too tired to go!"

Chris was so utterly exhausted that all she wanted was to go to bed. The sooner she got the kids settled, the sooner she could finish what she had to do so she could get into bed herself before she collapsed.

Finally, finished with the most pressing of her work, she dragged herself off to bed. She was so tired that she skipped her usual shower, promising herself she would take it in the morning when she felt better.

"Why did I accept that invitation? I'm sure I would feel so much better if I could just stay here tomorrow and rest," Chris asked herself as she tried, vainly, to find a comfortable position so her side would stop aching.

Chapter Two

The twins were so excited about the party that they were up at daylight the next morning begging Chris to get up long before her usual time. Finally, she gave up trying to sleep a little while longer and chased them out of her room so she could get dressed.

She wished for the hundredth time that she could call Cam and cancel the day, but Jon and Jenny were so excited that no matter how she felt, she couldn't disappoint them.

Sighing again, she threw back the covers and struggled out of bed. Maybe a hot shower would help.

The children were waiting impatiently for their breakfast when she finally got to the kitchen.

"Hurry up, Chris! We don't want to be late!" Jon exclaimed. "Besides we're hungry."

"Okay, you two. I'm hurrying as fast as I can." She smiled at their enthusiasm.

The shower had helped some, and the two cups of coffee she drank made her feel much better. As soon as breakfast was finished and the dishes done, Chris laid out clothes for the twins to wear. She generally let the children dress themselves, but they quite often didn't get everything right, so she always had to check their choices.

She didn't know what to wear. There wasn't anything very dressy in her wardrobe. After much indecision, she settled on her favorite: a long-sleeved navy and white gingham shirtwaist, with navy collar, cuffs, and belt. She slipped into a pair of white heels and changed to her white purse. This would have to do. A swift glance in the mirror told her that she was presentable.

She went to check on Jon and Jenny, only to find their rooms empty. She heard voices coming from the living room and found them both looking out the window.

"Come let me look at you." She checked their clothes and found Jenny had missed a button on her dress, and Jon had missed a belt loop on his pants. It was all she could do to get them to stand still for her to fix things.

"Isn't it time for him to come? Can you call Cam to be sure he didn't forget?" Jon voiced his fears.

"He'll be here," she promised.

"I must have been out of my mind to accept an invitation from a virtual stranger to heaven knows where, to a party where I won't know a soul. Worse yet, what do I tell the children if he doesn't show up? He's already five minutes late," Chris muttered to herself.

"It's five after ten. Where is he? You said he would be here at ten o'clock." Jenny fretted.

Chris was beginning to become angry. If he disappointed the kids she would . . . What could she do? She couldn't even call him because she didn't know how to get hold of him.

"It's him! He's here!" Jon shouted as he jerked the door open and rushed down the walk with Jenny in close pursuit.

Jon came to a sudden stop when he got a good look at the vehicle Cam was driving. It was the longest car he had ever seen!

"Where did you get that car?" He asked as soon as Cam came into sight around the back of it. "That's not the one you had yesterday."

"The one I had yesterday only had one seat. I don't think we all would have fit in it, so I brought this one. Do you think it will do?" Cam laughed at the expression on Jon's face.

"Are you ready for the party, Jenny?" he asked the little girl.

"Jon, Jenny, come get your sweaters," Chris called them back to the house before Jenny had a chance to answer.

Jon ran back for his sweater because he was anxious to look inside the car.

Jenny slipped her hand into Cam's extended one, and they went up the walk together. Chris was mildly surprised at this because it was completely out of character for her.

"Hurry up!" Jon allowed Chris to help him with his sweater only because it was faster that way.

"You haven't even said hello to Cam yet, have you? Where are your manners?" Chris scolded the impatient boy.

"Oh, I forgot. Hi, Cam," Jon said as he was on his way out the door again.

"Hello, Cam. We are awfully glad to see you again." This from Jenny as Chris helped her into her sweater.

"Good morning, Cam. As you may be able to tell, the kids are a little excited. I guess we had better go before one of them pops a button."

"How are you feeling this morning?" Cam asked as she stood before him. His eyes took in a lovely girl with the drawn look on her face and dark circles under her eyes. She looked so fragile that his heart went out to her. He renewed his promise to himself that he was going to find a way to help her, no matter what it took.

"I'm feeling much better." The intenseness of his look was a little unsettling for her, so she quickly turned to pick up the small gift she had wrapped the night before. It was a play makeup kit she had purchased a while back to give to Jenny sometime as a special gift. She hoped it would be suitable for a little girl who apparently had everything.

Cam waited as she closed and locked the door, then took her by the arm as they moved down the path. His touch burned her arm with a feeling she knew she would remember well. All too soon, they reached the car where Jon was circling, trying to see it from every angle.

"It sure is big," he said as he looked at the car.

"Would you like to see the inside of it?" Cam asked as he opened the rear door with a flourish. Jon scrambled in unceremoniously, but Jenny allowed him to assist her. When he had them both settled and their seat belts fastened, he closed the door and opened the front door for Chris.

"I'm sorry, I shouldn't have left you standing here while I tended to the kids. I should have gotten you settled first."

"Apology accepted. I always try to get them taken care of first anyway." He helped her in and closed the door when she was comfortable. On his way around the car he paused to check on the backseat passengers. Jenny hadn't moved at all, but Jon was stretching as far as his seat belt would allow so he could to look at everything.

He slid under the wheel, glancing at Chris as he did so. She was sitting quietly with her head resting against the back of the seat.

"You have a couple of really nice kids there." He wanted to ask about the parents, but that could wait. Maybe she would mention them on her own. If she didn't, he would still find out somehow.

"Thank you."

Curiosity had forced him to look through her billfold. He knew that he shouldn't have, but it was like someone else had control of his hands.

He found a picture of Chris, the twins, another girl he assumed to be Luci, and two adults.

He guessed the picture to be about three years old, judging by the kids' ages now. They all appeared to be a very happy, so what could have happened?

The driver's license told him that she was nineteen. Where were the parents? He hadn't seen a car, so perhaps they were just away on a trip for a few days.

"When are we going?" Jon's impatient voice brought Cam out of his thoughts. Patience was not one of Jon's virtues, especially since they were going to a party.

"Right now, son." Cam answered as he started the car, and with one last glance at Chris he put it in gear.

"Is everybody ready to have a good time today?" he asked as he pulled away from their house.

"Yes, we are!" the children answered in unison.

Sensing Chris's need for a few minutes to prepare for the day, he kept the children occupied by asking about their favorite classes in school and telling them about some of his experiences when he was in school.

Before she was ready, Chris felt the car slow down and make a turn off the road. She opened her eyes to see a long curved lane lined with trees. As the car made its way up the drive, she got her first glimpse of the house. It was a very large two-story brick with eight tall white columns around a portico on the front of it. Everywhere she looked there were flowers. Large urns filled with them lined the steps leading up to a set of double doors. The house was surrounded by a neatly manicured lawn with shrubs of all sizes and shapes. Chris had lived in Everett all of her life, but she had never seen this house.

In fact, she wasn't sure just where they were, but she doubted that it could be seen from the road. As the car came smoothly to a halt, she thought to herself, "Whoever lives here must be very wealthy." Not her kind of people at all, but for the children's sake she would do her best to fit in for the day.

Cam opened the rear door for the speechless children. Neither of them uttered a word as they slid out and stood by the car, looking at the biggest house they had ever seen.

He opened the front door for Chris. As she turned to slip out, strong arms gently pulled her to a standing position.

The front doors of the house opened, and a middle-aged uniformed woman came out to greet them.

"Hello, Ellen. Sorry if we're a little late. Is everyone else here?" Cam asked as he ushered his guests up the steps.

"Hello, Mr. Cam." Ellen beamed at him. "You're not late, but everybody is here. They're in the drawing room." Her eyes were drawn to the delicate-looking girl beside him and the silent children in front of her.

"Ellen, I would like you to meet Christine Walker, her brother Jon, and sister, Jenny." He slipped his arm around Chris's shoulders as she placed a hand on each head in front of her, to propel them forward to acknowledge the introduction.

"Ellen has been with the family for as long as I can remember." He smiled fondly at the older woman. "She claims she is just the house keeper, but that's not entirely true. She's a friend, companion, and caretaker of this family. We couldn't get along without her."

"Go on, Mr. Cam." Ellen blushed with embarrassment. "I just do my job."

"It's nice to meet you, Ellen." Chris was the first to find her tongue, and the twins followed with their own hi's.

"Hello, Miss Christine, it's nice to have you here."

"Hello, children. My, you two sure do look alike," Ellen bent and greeted the kids.

"We're twins," they answered in unison as they giggled. They liked being twins and loved announcing it to strangers.

"We had better go in. I'm sure little Miss Sarah is getting impatient for you to arrive." She turned to lead the way into the house.

They walked down a long hallway past at least four doors, according to Chris's count. At the end of the hall, she noticed another set of doors much like the ones they just entered through, only these were mostly glass.

She heard voices and laughter before they turned into the last opening to the left. She paused for a second to look at the people assembled there.

"Sarah!"

"Jenny!"

The little girls spotted each other at the same time, effectively breaking the ice for the newcomers. Everyone laughed at the reactions from the girls.

"This is Sarah, my new friend from school. The one I told you about yesterday," Jenny turned and explained to Chris.

"I'm very glad to meet you, Sarah. Is this your birthday?"

"Yes. I'm six years old today," Sarah answered. "My Grandma's giving me a party."

Cam slid his hand under Chris's elbow and urged her further into the room.

"Christine Walker, I would like for you to meet my family. From left to right, my sister Kathleen, her husband Robert, their son Bobby, and last but certainly not least, this lovely lady and hostess for the day, Ramona." Cam finished with a bow to Ramona.

"It's nice to meet you all. This is my brother Jon, and that's Jenny, in case you missed it earlier." She hoped she could remember all their names.

"We are all very casual around here, so just make yourself comfortable anywhere." Ramona rose and crossed the room to greet her newest guests.

"Thank you," Chris murmured as she sat down in the nearest chair.

"How is it that you got the day off, Cam?" Robert's voice was first to break the silence in the room as Ramona returned to her chair.

"I couldn't miss my only niece's birthday party. Besides, I deserve a day off once in a while," Cam responded as he settled in a chair as near as he could get to Chris.

"How are you progressing on the house?" Cam continued the conversation.

"Well, the work is going slow, but we really like what we have done so far. The first floor is just about finished, but I shudder every time I think about the condition of the upstairs," Kathleen filled Cam in.

Robert smiled at Kathleen, and than turned to include Chris. "We just recently moved here from Orlando."

"Actually, we bought the house last fall," Kathleen explained. "It was in real disrepair, but it had such possibilities that we couldn't turn it down. Besides it was the only house we could afford that was the size we wanted."

"We were going to renovate the whole house before we moved in, but we didn't count on the contractors' estimates being so high." Robert added, "So we decided to do as much of the work ourselves as we could, to save money."

"It didn't take long for us to decide it was too hard on us to work all day, drive up here, and work evenings and weekends." Kathleen grimaced at the thought of what they had gone through. "So we decided to fix up only enough space for us to be comfortable in. As soon as we could, we made the move. Now we can work as we feel like it and have the time and money."

"Bobby, why don't you take Jon out to see your new puppy?" Kathleen suggested.

The boys had been sitting quietly, eyeing each other curiously but not talking.

"Okay. Do you want to see her?" Bobby asked Jon. Both boys were very glad to escape the adults.

"May I, Chris?" Jon jumped up, ready to go with Bobby.

"Go ahead." Chris smiled at the eager boy. "Be careful, and try to keep your clothes clean."

"Come on! I'll show Walter to you." Both boys left as quickly as they could, before the adults thought of something else for them to do.

"Walter? I thought it was a female," Cam asked. "Where did he come up with Walter?"

"Well," Kathleen attempted to explain, "Walter was the name of his very best friend at the old school. They promised never to forget each other, so Bobby decided to name the puppy after him. We told him the puppy was a girl, but he said he didn't care."

"That's sweet," Chris ventured. "I guess if worse comes to worse, you can always call her Walterina." She laughed, timidly as everyone seemed to enjoy her attempt at humor.

"Mama, may Jenny and I go out and see the puppy too?" Sarah wanted to escape the watchful eyes of the adults also.

"If her sister doesn't mind." Kathleen left the decision to Chris.

"Just try not to get dirty." Chris allowed Jenny to go with Sarah.

Up until now, Ramona had been silent. She always enjoyed having guests in her home. It was pleasant listening to their conversations, but now it was time for her to take over her duties as hostess.

"It's nice to have you here, Christine. I appreciate you allowing Jon and Jenny to help Sarah celebrate her birthday. I'm afraid that I'm out of touch with the younger generation, so I just don't know any six-year-olds to invite to her party. When Cam mentioned meeting you yesterday, I was happy that he had asked you all to come here today."

"Thank you, Mrs.—" Chris paused unsure what to call her hostess.

"Please, just call me Ramona."

"Thank you, Ramona, and please do call me Chris. The twins don't get a chance to attend many parties, so I appreciate the opportunity for them to have a little extra fun in their lives."

"You have a beautiful house. I have always had an interest in interior design, and whoever did this room certainly knew what they were doing. It's very well done," Chris ventured. She had been discreetly admiring the décor since she first entered the room. It was at least three times the size of her living room. The huge floor to ceiling fireplace was the focal point of the room. It was constructed of black fieldstones held in place by light gray mortar. Randomly across the face, stones protruded from the front of the fireplace, so as to form shelves. On each shelf rested a brightly colored, life-sized porcelain bird, common to the area. Floor-to-ceiling windows flanked it. Each window had a venetian blind adjusted so as to defuse the bright Florida sunlight, and light gray sheer valances, the exact shade of the fireplace mortar, across the top.

Over to one side was a set of French doors opening out onto a veranda. Valences and blinds, matching the ones on the windows by the fireplace, opened to allow light from the shaded veranda to give the room an airy feeling.

The highly polished wood floor had darker multicolor but predominately gray area rugs placed strategically around the room.

The area in which they were seated consisted of a seven-foot dark red tweed sofa, where Robert and Kathleen sat; a large pale gray chair with matching ottoman, where Ramona was seated; and a pair of deep turquoise wingback chairs sharing an ottoman, where she and Cam were sitting.

A large round oak coffee table in the center seemed to tie everything together.

Two charcoal and gray tweed chairs, separated by a small lamp table, were located near the French doors, and against the far wall were an armoire and a side board. Off white walls gave the room a warm and cozy ambiance.

"Thank you, my dear. Cam's father had this house built ten years ago. I fell in love with it the first time I saw it, and I've been very comfortable here." Ramona smiled, a trifle sadly, Chris thought.

Ellen appeared at the door and stood as though waiting for instructions. Chris had not seen Ramona summon her, but apparently she had.

"Is every thing in order, Ellen?" Ramona asked as she rose to her feet.

"Yes, ma'am, everything is ready."

"Would you gather the children and see that they are presentable?"

She turned to Chris. "While we are waiting, would you like to see my rose garden? I think we will have plenty of time."

"I would love to," she answered, curious to see the back of the house.

"Have you always lived in Everett?" Ramona asked as she led the way onto the veranda.

"Yes, I have. In fact, in the same house. My father was an architect. He designed and built the house. My mother was an interior decorator by trade, so she did all the decorating. I guess that's where I got my interest in the subject."

"You speak of your parents in the past tense?" Ramona asked hesitantly.

"Three years ago my father had to fly to New York on business. It was only for a week, so my sister and I talked Mother into going with him. They hadn't had a vacation together in years, so we thought it would be nice for them. Luci, my sister, was eighteen, I was sixteen, and the twins were three. We promised to take care of each other until they returned. Except they didn't come back. They were both killed in a plane crash on the way home."

"I am so sorry. It's terribly hard to lose someone suddenly. Doubly so for your family because you were all so young." Ramona's heart went out to Chris. "I'm sorry. I didn't mean to dredge up unhappy memories." Ramona impulsively hugged Chris.

"I lost my husband in an accident not long ago, so I truly know how it feels to lose someone dear to you."

"Thank you. Now let's talk about more pleasant things. Like those beautiful roses." Chris thought it was time to change the subject.

"Those roses have been my salvation." Ramona beamed with pride as she led Chris for a closer look at the flower bed.

"Ellen won't allow me to lift a finger in the house." She looked over her shoulder as if checking to be sure Ellen wasn't around. "One time she caught me in 'her' kitchen, putting fresh shelf paper in a cabinet. She didn't say a word when she came in, but she didn't have to. I don't think I have ever seen such a look of disapproval on anyone's face in my life. Believe me, I didn't try that again!"

"It's a good thing she doesn't enjoy gardening." Ramona grinned as they came to a halt by the edge of the flower bed.

"They are the prettiest things I have ever seen!"

The bed was about thirty feet across. It was shaped like a wagon wheel with narrow walks where the spokes would have been. Each wedge was comprised of various shades of the same color with the lightest shades near the center and turning progressively darker as they fanned out to the outer edge. A large three-tiered fountain filled the center, and a low brick wall circled the outside. A small shaded seating area, off to one side, provided the perfect place to rest and enjoy the beauty of the garden.

"I've never seen so many shades of the colors. Where on earth did you find them, and how did you come to build a round bed like this?" Chris asked.

"I saw a picture in a book when I was a little girl and promised myself that someday I would have a flower bed like it. It's taken me nearly ten years of combing catalogs and visiting nurseries to locate all these colors. Now, I spend time out here every day. My children have grown up and don't need me much anymore, so I guess I have, in a sense, let these become their replacements. I worry about them when it gets too cool, if it rains too much, or when the wind blows too hard. I know it's silly, but they make me feel needed, and that's important to me." Ramona stood silently, gazing at her beloved flowers, lost in memories.

"We all need to be important to someone," Chris gently agreed. "For me, it's my little brother and sister. I've mostly cared for them since they were three. My older sister has been working most of the time and hasn't really had the time that I have had to spend with them."

"It couldn't have been easy for any of you. It's hard enough for children to grow up with parents sometimes, let alone without them.

Trying to be both mother and father to them must have been almost more than you could handle at times," Ramona sympathized.

"Sometimes, you do what you have to do without thinking of how hard it is. We have managed all right," Chris answered.

"Well, enough about us and our problems! I expect that we have some impatient children awaiting our return," Ramona changed the subject, much to Chris's relief.

Chris, anxious to talk about happier things, led the way back into the house. They found the room they had just left empty.

"Well, I guess they are ready to start things with or without us," Ramona commented as she led Chris to a room beside the staircase leading to the second floor. The room had balloons and crepe paper everywhere. A large banner wishing Sarah a happy sixth birthday was hanging on the wall, and below it was a table decorated with fairytale characters and loaded with brightly covered packages.

Jon and Bobby were seated together over by the far wall, trying not to look too interested but not so far away as to miss anything. Sarah and Jenny were standing beside the decorated table.

"My stars! Look at all those packages, Sarah!" Ramona exclaimed as they entered the room.

"Can I start opening them now, Grandma? Please." Sarah had been patient long enough.

"I guess so if everyone else is ready." She looked around the room to see if everyone was there. Robert and Cam were deep in conversation off to the side.

"All right, you two. No more shop talk this afternoon!" she scolded them.

Kathleen gathered one man on each arm and marched them to chairs near the table where Sarah had begun opening her packages.

Jenny had backed away from the table, but she hadn't taken her eyes off it. Chris was sure she couldn't understand why Sarah had so many packages when she and Jon only got one apiece for their last birthday. Luci had forgotten all about it, so all they got was something from Chris.

"Mama, can Jenny help me open some of these presents?" Sarah asked when she looked around and saw Jenny watching.

"Of course she may. In fact, if we look around, I think there just might be a package for her, and there could even be one for Bobby and another for Jon." Kathleen checked the packages, looking for special ones.

Jenny's eyes lit up, and the two boys sprang to their feet, suddenly very much interested in the goings on.

"It's tradition in our family," Ramona interrupted when Chris started to object. "Every one who comes to a birthday party takes something home."

Kathleen handed the boys identically wrapped packages, which they immediately tore into as only small boys can.

The box she presented to Jenny was pink with a frilly bow. Very carefully, Jenny pulled the bow off and removed the box lid. Her eyes fairly sparkled when she saw the contents.

"Chris! Look! It's my very own baby doll!" She gently lifted the doll from its box. Hugging it tightly, she gleefully danced over to show it to Chris.

The boys found remote controlled cars in their packages.

"Come see what I got, Chris!" Jon was just as excited as Jenny, but he was trying not to show it because he thought himself too grownup for that.

The boys made no pretense of watching Sarah any longer because they were too busy seeing how their cars worked to be bothered with anything else.

Robert and Cam helped the boys get the cars ready for action.

Sarah received a doll much like the one Jenny had and several other little-girl gifts, but the gift that Chris brought seemed to be her favorite.

"They seem to be enjoying themselves." Chris jumped as Cam's voice broke into her thoughts. "Now aren't you glad you came?"

"I will admit that at first I had some reservations, but now I am glad that we are here. Jon and Jenny don't get to do this very often. I'm sure this is all they will talk about for days to come," Chris conceded.

"I really appreciate your allowing the children to come today," Kathleen joined the conversation. "They all seem to get along well together. Bobby is at the age when he sometimes ignores his little sister, so once in a while she gets lonely up here. I thought a real birthday party might cheer her up, but I'm not sure just how much fun she would have had with only us old fogies here. Jenny has definitely cheered her up."

"Chris, do you live near here?" Kathleen asked.

"I have to admit, I'm not exactly sure where we are, but our house is just a little ways east of the Eastland factory," Chris replied.

"That's great! We live in the northeast part of town, so our houses probably aren't too far apart. I hope you will allow the twins to come over and play sometimes this summer," Kathleen asked hopefully.

As soon as Sarah was finished opening her gifts, Ellen cleared the table and promptly refilled it with assorted picnic items. There were hamburgers, hotdogs, sliced ham, potato salad, cole slaw, baked beans, and various other items for an indoor picnic. Chris forced herself to eat though she wasn't the least bit hungry. She was so tired that all she really wanted was for the day to end so she could go back to the quiet of her little house.

As soon as the meal was finished, Ellen cleared the table to make room for the dessert.

She reentered the room pushing a cart loaded with a huge decorated cake accompanied by a freezer of ice cream.

Ramona lit the six candles perched on top of the cake, and after making a wish, Sarah blew them all out in one try.

After the children were seated and supplied with cake and ice cream, the adults filled their plates. Chris perched on the edge of the settee, balancing her plate on her knees. Cam took a seat beside her. A tingle ran up her leg when his leg brushed against hers as he made himself comfortable with his plate.

"This cake is so good, it has to be homemade." She felt obligated to say something to her seatmate. "In fact, everything here has been delicious."

"Knowing Ellen, I'm sure that everything we've had today has been home made. And yes, everything I've seen is delectable," Cam agreed, looking at Chris in a way that made her feel that it wasn't only the food he was talking about.

"Ellen is known far and wide for her cooking abilities," Kathleen joined in on the conversation. "We've tried every way we know how to talk her into getting some help with the housework because we think it's getting to be too much for her. She adamantly refuses. She says it would be easier to do it herself than to follow someone else around and redo everything."

She looked around to be sure Ellen wasn't within earshot and then continued. "She's getting on in years, but we don't dare suggest that's why we think she needs help."

"Surely, when she gets to the point that she needs a little help, she won't be too proud to ask for it," Chris reasoned.

Many times she had felt overwhelmed with her job, night school, housework, and the twins. Up until now, she had always been able to surmount her difficulties. This time she wasn't sure if she could or not. Well, that wasn't exactly true. She would manage, but it would be a serious disappointment if she had to drop out of school again. Her parents had died between her junior and senior year of high school. Chris felt the twins needed her more than she needed school, so she stayed home to care for them. Luci had graduated the year before, and she was too busy preparing for her own future to have time for her siblings.

Chris promised herself to someday go back and get her high school diploma. When she turned eighteen, she went to work at Eastland. She used part of her salary to pay a babysitter for the twins so she could go to night school to get her diploma. As soon as she did that, she enrolled in some college courses to work on a degree in interior decorating. For now, it was looking like she would have to give up that dream.

Chris sighed heavily, unaware that both Kathleen and Cam had ceased talking and were watching her expression with concerned eyes.

Cam had related to Kathleen and Ramona what little he knew about Chris and why he had really invited the three of them to the party. He also warned them against offering any sort of help outright. He was determined to help, but he had yet to figure out a way to do so without offending her pride.

"Come, children, it's time to go home," Chris called to the twins. Her side was beginning to ache again, and she was growing extremely tired.

"Oh, Chris, do we have to?" Jon was reluctant to leave his new friend.

"Please, we would love for you to stay a while longer, if you can," Ramona spoke up on Jon's behalf.

"That's very kind of you, but I'm really tired, so I think it will be better if we go home now. That is, if Cam will take us." She turned to Cam, hoping he would agree.

"If that's what you want, of course I will," Cam answered quietly.

"Before you go, Chris, would you give me your phone number? I would like to call you if it's all right." Kathleen handed her a pad and pencil. "Perhaps we can get together with the children sometime soon. I've written my number down for you, so please call. I would like to keep in touch. I really don't know anyone yet. It would be so nice to have someone to talk to about something other than business for a change."

Jon and Jenny bid sad farewells to their new friends. They each were promised that they would be able to see each other soon.

"I'm so very glad you came today, my dear." Ramona slipped her arm around Chris as they walked to the car. "It made Sarah very happy to have a friend of her own age here."

"I appreciate your thoughtfulness. Jon and Jenny don't get to go to parties very often."

Chris thanked her hostess.

"Children, have you thanked Ramona for your gifts?" She turned to the twins to remind them of their manners.

"Oh, we forgot," Jon apologized for the both of them. "Thank you for our presents. We really like them."

"Thank you," Jenny added as she clutched her new doll.

"You both are quite welcome, and I want you to come back and see me very soon." Ramona bent to hug the children. Jenny slipped her arm around Ramona's neck and gave her a shy hug. Jon allowed a short hug before turning to scramble into the car as soon as he was free.

Ramona smiled as she straightened up, not missing Jon's reluctance for a hug. She turned to Chris and Kathleen, standing beside her. "I don't believe Jon likes to be hugged any more than Bobby does."

"No, I'm afraid he's growing up," Chris agreed.

"Bobby runs like a rabbit if he thinks someone is on the verge of trying to touch him. Heaven forbid if his mother wants to kiss him." Kathleen shook her head as she laughed.

"Please, do come back." Ramona bid them good-bye as Cam assisted Chris into the car, closed the door, and went around to take his seat behind the wheel.

"Good-bye, everyone. We enjoyed ourselves very much. Thank you, again for everything," Chris responded, thankful to be going back to the quiet of her little home.

Chapter Three

On the way home, Chris thought about the people she had met that day.

Robert and Kathleen seemed made for each other. They had such a relaxed manner when they were around each other that Chris felt a pang of sadness. In some ways they reminded her of her parents. They were comfortable to be around, and laughter seemed to follow them. Kathleen told her that they had been married for eight years and that Cam had not yet married.

Ramona was every bit a lady, from her honey-blonde hair swirled into a French roll to her expensively clad feet. At first, Chris thought she was very aloof, but after their talk by the rose bed, she decided that Ramona was merely reserved, maybe a little sad. She hadn't said how her husband died nor how long ago, but Chris suspected that time was unimportant to her. Widowhood would probably rest heavily upon her for the rest of her life.

Chris had intended to watch how they went home so she could figure out where Ramona lived, but she was so lost in thought that they were pulling up in front of her house before she knew it.

"Kids, did you have a good time today?" Cam asked as he opened the door to let them out of the car.

"Oh yes," Jenny was the first to answer. "I just love my doll, and I'm going to keep her forever."

"I've never had a car like this. It's great!" Jon held it up so Cam could see it again.

"And how was your day?" he asked Chris as he helped her out of the car.

"It was very pleasant. You were right when you said I would like your sister. She is very nice, and I enjoyed talking with her."

"I'm glad you went. I—Sarah was very pleased to have guests at her party. I hope you and the kids will visit us again before too long. Ramona rarely has company, so I'm sure she sometimes gets very lonely." Cam paused in front of Chris. He was very reluctant to have the day end. He still didn't have a clue as to how he could help her.

"Well—I guess I had better get the door unlocked. The children are waiting. Thank you for everything. You have a very pleasant family, and you've certainly made an impression on the twins." Chris was almost sorry to see him leave.

"Then, I guess I'll say good-bye for now." After a moment, he released her arm and watched as she and the twins moved up the walk to their front door before turning to get back into his car.

"Go take off your good clothes," Chris urged the children as she went to change hers. After donning jeans, a shirt, and sneakers, she quickly made out a grocery list, including only the things that they really needed in order to save as much money as she could.

As soon as the twins were ready, they walked to the grocery store a few blocks away. She wished she still had the car. She had gotten her drivers license on her sixteenth birthday and had been using her father's car while they had it. Luci took it to New York when she went there last year. She borrowed some money from Chris to make the trip. She was so sure of finding a job that she sold the car so she could stay a few more days. Nothing came of it, so she had come home on the bus, promising to get a job so she could buy another car for them.

By the time they returned, each carrying a bag, the pain in her side was intense. She barely had the strength to put the groceries away.

The twins were in their rooms playing with their new toys, so Chris took the opportunity to lie down to rest for a little while. A short nap would help, she was sure.

Before she opened her eyes she felt someone staring at her. When she looked she found two sets of eyes watching her. "We didn't think you were ever going to wake up. We're hungry. Can we eat pretty soon?" Jon complained.

Groggily she looked at the clock. It was six thirty! She had been asleep for well over an hour. She had only intended to take a short nap before she fixed dinner!

"No wonder you're hungry. It's long past time to eat." Chris felt a little better as she hurried to the kitchen to fix something for them to eat. "Go wash your hands while I go see what we have."

She had some leftover beef stew, so she heated that, sliced a tomato, and warmed up some creamed corn. That would have to do.

"Can we go outside and play after we get through supper?" Jon asked.

"We'll see." It was beginning to get dark, so she doubted if they could, but she didn't feel like listening to them complain if she said no. Chris wasn't hungry, so she just had a cup of coffee to keep the youngsters company while they ate.

The doorbell rang just as they were finishing. When Chris went to the door, she was surprised to see Cam standing there with two sweaters in his hand.

"I thought you might need these." He grinned as he handed them to her.

"I seem to be making a habit of leaving things in your car. I'm not usually that absent minded," she apologized as she took the sweaters.

The ringing of the telephone interrupted them.

"Do come in and excuse me for a moment, please."

"Hi, Sis. It's me." Luci was on the other end.

"Luci! Where are you?"

"I'm staying at Frank's apartment for now. Do you have a pencil? I'm going to give you his address and phone number so you can send my things. It's kind of crowded here, so I'm going to have find my own place as soon as I can."

"When are you going to look for a job?" Chris asked after she had taken the information down and slipped it into her pocket for safe keeping.

"I'll look for one just as soon as I get moved into my own place. I don't like it here. I have to sleep on the couch," Luci complained. "I need my things as soon as possible. I could use some extra money so I can get an apartment. I think three hundred ought to get me started."

"I don't have that kind of money, Luci! I need every thing I have to get by until I find another job," Chris tried to explain. She would have given anything if Cam had not been standing there listening to every word she said.

"But, Chris, I can't stay here! It's too crowded!" Luci insisted.

"I'm sorry, Luci, but that's the way it has to be."

The phone went dead as an angry Luci slammed the receiver down.

Chris was very nearly in tears as she quietly replaced the receiver in its cradle.

As she turned to face a curious Cam, everything went black. Cam caught her in his arms before she fell to the floor.

When she opened her eyes she was on her bed. A wet towel had been placed across her forehead. Jon and Jenny were standing wide-eyed at the foot of the bed, and Cam was bending over her.

She was embarrassed to have fainted, but she felt too wretched to do anything more than just lie there. Then she thought about how it must have frightened the twins and struggled to a sitting position.

"I'm all right," she assured the children. "I just need to lie here and rest for a few minutes," she added as she dropped her head back on the pillow and closed her eyes.

"Will you be all right for a little bit?" Cam asked her.

"Of course, I'll be all right. I just turned around too fast and got a little dizzy."

She heard Cam say something to the kids, and then they all left the room.

"Are you feeling any better?" Cam had quietly reentered the room.

"Much better. I told you I would be fine in a few minutes." Chris forced a smile to convince him.

"I just spoke to Ramona, I told her what happened, and she insists that I bring all of you back to her house. I'm going to help the kids get some of their stuff together, then I will be back to pack some things for you." Cam pressed her back down on the bed when she attempted to sit up.

"I told you I will be fine. All I need is a good night's rest," Chris protested. "There's no need for you to go to all this trouble just for us."

"You are in no shape to be left alone. I will feel much better if I know there's someone to look after you. Now, lie there until I get back. That's an order!" He didn't sound like he was used to being disobeyed, so she didn't object.

In a short time he returned to her room to collect a few of her things. When he finished, he carried her case out of the room.

"Are you okay?" Jenny slipped up to the bed.

"Yes, sweetie, I'm just a little tired," Chris tried to reassure the worried little girl.

"Cam says that we are going to stay at Ramona's for a few days," Jenny informed her.

"He helped Jon and me get some of our clothes and stuff. Can I take my new doll with me?" she asked.

"Of course you may. It might be fun to stay there tonight, don't you think? We'll probably come back home tomorrow," Chris explained.

"I guess if you will be there too. Where is Luci? Will she know where to find us?"

"Luci had to leave for a few days." She had been hoping her sister would change her mind and come home, so she hadn't mentioned where Luci was. "I have her phone number, so I can call and tell her where we are."

Jenny was quiet for a moment and then asked, "She didn't tell us good-bye. Doesn't she want to live with us anymore?"

"She wanted to tell you good-bye, but she didn't have time. She told me to say good-bye and to give each of you a hug and kiss. I guess I forgot. I'm sorry. She is coming back as soon as she can," Chris lied in an effort to make the little girl feel better.

"Everything's in the car, and I checked to see that all the doors and windows are closed and locked. Shall we go?" Cam had returned to the bedroom to help Chris.

She started to get up, but Cam's hand on her shoulder stopped her movement.

"Take it easy. You shouldn't try to do that. I'm going to carry you to the car." Cam bent to slip his arms under her.

"I can walk. Please let me. The kids are frightened enough without you carrying me. I promise to lean on you if you will just let me walk," Chris pleaded.

"I guess, maybe you are right." Cam straightened back up and offered his hand to assist her to her feet.

He slipped his arm around her shoulder to steady her for a moment before they started across the floor. She was weaker than she thought, so she slipped her arm around his waist for support.

"Can you get the door for us, Jon?" Cam asked as they slowly made their across the living room.

Jenny followed, not taking her eyes off of Chris. Her sister was never sick, so she didn't know what to think, but somehow she knew that if she stayed near Chris, everything would be all right.

Jon took Jenny's hand as they followed the adults slowly down the walk to the car.

After installing Chris in the front seat and the kids in the back seat, Cam quickly traced his steps to the house to lock the door, and then hurriedly returned to the car.

Ramona and Ellen were waiting at the door when the car pulled up in front of the house.

Ellen quickly took charge of the children while Cam and Ramona tended to Chris.

"Take her upstairs, Cam. I've prepared the room at the head of the stairs." Ramona directed him. "Where are the suitcases?"

"In the trunk," Cam answered as he tossed her the keys.

"You go ahead. I'll be along shortly to put her to bed." Ramona sent them on their way before Chris fainted again.

Earlier in the day, Chris had wondered where the stairs went. She didn't expect to ever find out, and certainly not in this way.

Cam was almost carrying her by the time they got to the bedroom. Pure grit had kept her going, or pride. Either way, she was determined not to faint again. With a sigh, she sank down on the bed, thankful she didn't have any farther to go. Her side was aching terribly. She rubbed it, trying to ease the pain, and groaned softly. The movement did not go unnoticed.

"Are you in pain?"

"No, I'm fine." Chris didn't want to cause any more trouble to Cam's family.

"I don't believe you. Tell me the truth," Cam demanded.

"Well, my side does hurt a little," she conceded.

"How long has it been bothering you?"

"Off and on, I guess for about a month," Chris answered quietly.

"Okay, Cam, you can go now," Ramona broke into their conversation as she entered the room. "I want to get Chris settled into bed. Would you bring up the children's things and put them in the room across the hall? They might be happier if they share a room close to their sister for tonight at least."

"We'll talk again later." Cam turned back to Chris before he left.

As soon as Cam was out of the room, Ramona stood for a moment looking at the pale, fragile girl in front of her.

"Let's get you comfortable, my dear," Ramona said as she opened the case she had carried in and removed a night gown for Chris.

While she was doing this, Chris stood up by the side of the bed. She was feeling a little better and more than a little foolish for having caused all this trouble. She had never fainted in her life. Why did she have to do it in front of a man who had already gone so far out of his way to help her? He must think she was a hopeless case! And the twins! They must be scared to death!

"Where are Jon and Jenny?" Chris asked. "I have to see them so I can tell them I'm okay."

"Ellen has them under her wing. I'm sure they are well taken care of. If it will make you feel better, I'll see that they come up to see you in a little while. But first, let's get you into this gown and under the covers. Do you feel up to doing it yourself, or would you like me to stay and help?"

"I can manage." Chris offered a weak smile to show Ramona she was feeling better.

"Very well. While you are doing that, I will go down and check on the children. I'll bring you up some hot tea after you get settled."

As soon as she was alone, Chris quickly donned the ruffled gown Ramona had laid on the bed and slipped between the soft sheets. The bed felt like heaven. She was so much weaker than she thought.

Just as she got comfortable, she heard a sharp rap on the door.

"Come in." She expected it to be Ramona with the tea.

"Are you decent?" A male voice called out as the door cracked open a moment before it opened wide, to reveal Cam holding a tray.

"Jon said you didn't eat anything for supper, so I thought you should have something before you went to sleep."

He waited until she struggled to a sitting position while trying to keep the sheet from falling down. He smothered a smile as he loosened the sheet at the foot of the bed so she could pull it up far enough to allow her to sit up straight for the tray to fit over her lap.

"Are you comfortable?" Cam asked as he positioned the tray in front of her and tucked a napkin under the collar of her gown.

Chris was sure she wouldn't be able to eat a bite, until she saw the potato soup. It was her favorite. She had to at least try it. Before she realized it, the bowl was empty. She would have to ask Ellen if she would give her the recipe because it was by far the best soup she had ever tasted. Strawberry Jell-O with pineapple finished her meal. Once she got started, she couldn't seem to stop until it was all gone.

Cam sat quietly as she ate, and all the while she was being very careful to keep the sheet tucked closely under her chin. It had been a long while since he had seen a girl with so much modesty. Whether he would admit it or not, he was more drawn to her each time they met. He noted some of the color had returned to her cheeks. A good night's sleep would probably do her a world of good.

He certainly would like to have a word with Luci! He would bet anything he had that she was the cause of most of Chris's problems.

"Are you feeling better?" he asked as she drank the last of her hot tea.

"Much better. How could I not after eating that wonderful soup?" Chris laughed softly.

"Back to your side, how does it feel?" he asked, watching her closely. He had figured out that she wasn't a very good liar, so he knew he could tell if she were not truthful.

"Actually, it feels pretty good. I told you that all I needed was a little rest. Some of Ellen's marvelous cooking has certainly helped." Chris denied the tenderness she still felt.

"Okay, I'll take that for now. In the meantime I think there are a couple of kids waiting to see you. Do you feel up to it?" Cam asked. He didn't completely believe her, but he decided to drop the subject, for now. They certainly would have to discuss it again before he was going to allow her to go back home.

"Of course, I want to see them!" Chris exclaimed.

Cam removed the tray from the bed and allowed to twins to enter the room as he took the tray downstairs, to give them some privacy.

They both stopped just inside the door, not quite sure what to do.

"Come here, you two, I need a hug." Chris opened her arms for both of them.

Relieved, the youngsters broke into wide grins and rushed for the bed. They didn't stop until they were both safely enfolded in their big sister's arms.

"I'm sorry if I worried you. I just got a little tired, that's all. Ramona wants us to spend the night here, if that's all right with both of you." Chris tried to calm their fears.

"Are you sure you are okay?" Jenny wasn't completely satisfied.

"I promise you, I am okay. All I need is a good night's sleep." Chris squeezed the both of them as tightly as she could.

Satisfied, the children sat on the bed and told Chris what they had been doing.

"We really like Ellen," Jon said. "She tells funny stories about when she was little. That must have been a long time ago because I think she is probably older than you are." Chris tried her best not to smile at the seriousness of Jon's observation.

"She gave us some ice cream and another piece of Sarah's birthday cake," Jenny added.

Ramona quietly entered the room and paused just inside the door to take in the sight before her. Their love for each other was so obvious that at that moment she would have gladly traded places with any one of them.

"Would you children like to see your room?" she asked as she made her presence known. "It's just across the hall from here." She thought it was time for Chris to get some rest, so she was going to keep the kids busy until bedtime.

Chris settled back on her pillow after everyone had gone. She decided a nap sounded like a good idea.

The sun, streaking across her face, woke her. For a moment, she couldn't remember where she was, and then the events of the evening before came flooding back. She didn't see a clock in the room, but the sun was high in the sky. It must be nearly noon! Where were the twins? She had better get up and find them.

After a quick wash in the bathroom, she dressed in the clothes she had worn the night before and went in search of her brother and sister. The room across from hers was empty, so she descended the stairs. The only sounds she heard led her to the kitchen, and the aroma of food reminded her that she was starving.

"Good morning." Chris found Ellen standing at the stove. "I'm looking for Jon and Jenny. Have you seen them?"

"Oh yes, Miss Christine. They are out by the pool with Bobby and Sarah. Mrs. Ramona and Mrs. Kathleen are watching over them. Mr. Cam has gone out for a while, but before he left he told me to be sure you ate a good breakfast when you got up." Ellen bustled about preparing a plate of food for her.

"Please, don't go to any trouble for me. Coffee will do just fine," Chris protested, but not too strongly because she really was hungry.

"It's no trouble at all, Miss Christine. Please sit down." She motioned to a table in front of a bay window, off to the side of the kitchen. "I'll have this ready in no time. Don't worry about those youngsters because they are doing just fine."

Ellen put a plate of food in front of Chris in short order. There was ham, scrambled eggs, hash browns, and toast. She added orange juice and coffee.

Chris normally didn't eat much breakfast, but this time she devoured the whole plate of food. She couldn't remember the last time anyone had fixed her breakfast. She was always the one to do the cooking and cleaning up afterwards.

"That was the nicest breakfast I've had in a long time, Ellen. Thank you," Chris expressed her gratitude. "I will be happy to wash the dishes before I leave."

"Good heavens, no! You go find the children. I can manage a few extra things," Ellen shooed her out of the kitchen.

She heard the excited laughter before she found the children. All four of them were in the wading pool, splashing water on each other. Ramona and Kathleen were on lounge chairs, watching, but making sure they were out of the way of errant water drops.

"Come join us." Kathleen was the first to see her. "It's a beautiful day."

"How are you feeling?" Ramona turned to look at Chris.

"I'm feeling much better. Thank you," Chris replied as she took a seat near the two women.

Just as she sat down, Jon spotted her and promptly forgot about the water game. He went charging toward Chris with Jenny right behind him. Chris slipped out of the chair onto her knees, with both arm wide so both could be hugged at once. No one seemed to mind that she was getting soaked in the process.

Kathleen and Ramona exchanged smiles at the sight before them. Jon and Jenny couldn't possibly know just how lucky they were to have someone who cared for them as much as Chris obviously did.

"The poor dear had been mother and father for those tykes for most of their lives. It's no wonder she's all tuckered out," Ramona murmured. "Her sister should be sharing the responsibility, but from what Cam said, I guess she is no help at all. I don't understand why that is."

"I would certainly like to have a few words with that Luci!" Kathleen fumed quietly, so as not to be overheard. Cam had told them about the phone calls Chris had received while he was at her house.

When the twins stepped away from Chris to tell her what they had been doing, Ramona handed her a towel. "Dry off with this, dear. You look as though you have been in the pool with the children." Ramona chuckled as she looked at the drenched girl.

"I guess I am a little bit damp." Chris dried off as best she could. "I appreciate all that you have done for us, but I think we should be going home pretty soon."

"Oh please," Kathleen pleaded. "The children are having such a good time that I hate to stop them. Couldn't you stay until after lunch?"

"Besides, Cam gave me strict instructions to keep you here until he got home," Ramona explained why Chris needed to stay a little while longer. "I think he just wants to see for himself that you are feeling better. That's all."

"I'm fine, really. I promise to rest when I get home." Chris knew she should leave before having to face Cam again, but what could it hurt to have lunch? "They look as though they are having such a good time playing together. I guess it wouldn't hurt to have lunch before we go."

"If you want to go take a nap, we will be happy to keep an eye on the children," Ramona suggested when she saw Chris try unsuccessfully to smother a yawn. "It's always a pleasure to watch children at play."

"If you're sure you don't mind, I believe I will take you up on your offer. That huge breakfast that Ellen fixed me and this warm sun has made me a little sleepy." Chris yawned again. "All I need is a few minutes, and I will feel fine."

Her head barely touched the pillow before she was sound asleep.

Ramona allowed the twins to look in on her to see where she was, and Cam stopped by to see her. He tiptoed into the room, stood silently for a moment watching her sleep. Gently he pulled the blanket over her shoulder, smoothed her hair out of her face, and then quietly left her to sleep.

Chris was just trying to wake up when Kathleen next looked in on her.

"What time is it?" Chris asked, groggy from her sleep.

"It's a little before four," Kathleen answered as she entered the room. "How are you feeling?"

"I think I feel fine," Chris answered, trying to clear her head. "I can't believe I slept all afternoon. I don't generally get to nap in the daytime because there always seems to be something that has to be done."

"I was hoping you felt rested because there's something I need to ask you." Kathleen smiled, hopeful. "It's a huge favor, and I can't blame you if you say no, but please hear me out first."

"What is it?" Chris wondered what she could possibly do for Kathleen.

"Well, there is this play at the local theater that Cam has really wanted to see. He was able to get tickets yesterday for a performance tonight. He was going to take Mother, Robert, and me. It turns out that Robert had some clients come into town unexpectedly today for a meeting tomorrow, so we are committed to entertaining them tonight, and Mother has promised to take care of the kids for us," Kathleen explained.

"That's too bad. It sounds like it would have been a nice evening," Chris sympathized with her. "But where do I come in?"

"It's very difficult to get tickets, and they are only good for tonight." Kathleen took a deep breath and continued, "I know, as much as Cam wants to see the play, he won't go alone. So would you consider accompanying him tonight so all the tickets won't go to waste?"

"I couldn't possibly! We have to go home this evening. There's school for the children tomorrow, besides I don't have anything dressy enough to wear somewhere like that."

"I just wish—" What she wouldn't give to be able to say yes.

A knock at the door cut Chris short.

"Come in," she called.

Cam stuck his head in the door. "I wondered if you were feeling better." He was relieved to see how much better she looked than when he last saw her. He turned to Kathleen. "Have you talked to her yet?"

"Yes she has, but I just can't go." Chris regretted her answer more than she liked to admit. "I have to get the kids home so they will be ready for school tomorrow."

"I've been thinking about that." Cam turned back to Kathleen. "Bobby and Sarah go to the same school as Jon and Jenny, don't they?"

"Yes." She understood what he was getting at and agreed with him.

"Bobby and Sarah are already spending the night here, so why can't Jon and Jenny do the same? I can take them all to school in the morning," Cam pleaded his case with Chris.

"If you don't want to spend the night here, I will take you home after the play."

"The children don't have their school clothes."

"I'm sure we can find clothes for them," Kathleen countered, sensing Chris was weakening.

"I don't have anything to wear."

"I think I can help you out with that problem," Kathleen answered thoughtfully. "We're about the same size, so I'm sure I can find something that will work among the clothing I have stored here while we're renovating."

"It seems that I'm out numbered," Chris answered after a moment. "I'll need to talk to the children first, and if it's okay with them to stay here tonight, I guess I will take you up on your offer."

"If you want, I'll talk to the kids. I'm sure they won't mind when they find out Bobby and Sarah will be here too," Cam offered.

"I expect that you're right, so if you want to, I guess it'd be okay."

Chris was elated to have a chance to see a real live play in a theater, but she tried not to show too much excitement.

"I have reservations for dinner before the theater, so we'll have to leave about six. Can you have her ready by then?" Cam asked Kathleen. He was a little surprised and more than a little relieved that Chris had agreed to go with him. This would give him a chance to try to get more information about her and her family.

"She will be ready!" Kathleen was really glad this worked out because she thought they made a good pair. Maybe they would see that also if they spent some time alone together. Only time would tell.

"Are you sure you feel up to this evening?" Cam was giving Chris one last chance to back out if she truly didn't feel like going out tonight.

"Oh, yes! I feel fine!" Chris couldn't remember the last time she had gone out for an evening without the twins. She would worry about her future tomorrow, but just for tonight, she wanted to enjoy herself and not even think about anything else.

"Okay, Kathleen, she is in your hands. Work your magic." With that Cam took his leave. Kathleen sent Chris to take a bubble bath while she went to select some dresses for her to try on.

After soaking in the lavender scented bath until she felt like a prune, Chris donned the plush terry robe hanging on the back of the door and set about shampooing her hair. When she finished, she wrapped her head in a towel and went in search of Kathleen. She found her in a room down the hall, sorting out clothing. There were four dresses lying across the bed. One, a beautiful shimmering blue, caught her attention immediately.

"Are you ready to try on clothes?" Kathleen turned from the stack of lingerie she had been sorting through when Chris came in the room.

"They are so beautiful!" Chris exclaimed.

"We'll try them all on, and then decide which one is the best." Kathleen helped her pick out some lingerie and then left so she could trade her robe for the foundation garments in order for her to try on the long gowns.

After trying them all on, the gown Kathleen decided looked the best was the one that had first drawn Chris's interest.

After Chris put on her makeup, Kathleen styled her hair into an old-fashioned French roll with tendrils hanging around the back of her neck and in front of each ear. When that was finished, she let Kathleen help her slip into the dress again. She hardly recognized herself when she looked at her reflection in a full-length mirror.

At five minutes before six, Kathleen followed a very nervous Chris down to where Cam was waiting.

By the time they reached the bottom of the stairs, Cam was standing there absolutely dumbfounded! This couldn't be the same girl he had helped up the stairs twenty-four hours ago!

She was stunning! The dress was a sapphire blue watered silk with delicate white lace trimming the high neckline and narrow waist. The arm openings were cut so as to expose each shoulder, and a pleated skirt fell gracefully to the floor, concealing matching heels. She was carrying a silver lame shawl in case it got cool later in the evening.

Ramona stood to greet the couple as they went in to say good night.

"You look lovely, child," Ramona assured a nervous Chris.

"I think I'm jealous." Kathleen grimaced. "That dress didn't look nearly that good on me."

"It's the prettiest dress I have ever seen," Chris admitted.

"Well, I guess we had better go," Cam finally got his voice back. He took Chris by the arm, preparing to escort her to the waiting car.

"Have a good evening, children," Ramona bade them good night.

"I'm sure we will," Cam answered. "At least I know I will because I'll have the prettiest girl there on my arm."

"Now you're embarrassing me," Chris protested.

"I'm sorry. I truly didn't mean to do that. Please forgive me. Shall we go?" Cam apologized as he escorted her from the room.

Chapter Four

A different car was waiting in front of the house. A uniformed driver opened the rear car door for them. She wondered briefly just how many cars Cam owned. This was the third that she had seen.

Cam looked so handsome in his tuxedo as they walked down the steps to the waiting white limo that Chris felt like a princess going to the ball with the prince. She slid into the rear seat and felt a burning sensation shoot through her body when his thigh brushed hers as he settled beside her on the seat.

"Have you ever eaten at Ivanhoe's?" He was first to break the silence.

"No, I haven't. But I've heard of it. It's supposed to have very good food." Chris rarely got to eat out and never at expensive restaurants, as she was sure this place would be.

"The food is excellent. They serve most any sort of food, but they specialize in seafood and chicken," Cam explained what she could expect in the line of food.

She ventured a sideways look at her companion for the evening and immediately wished she hadn't because he was studying her. When their eyes met it was as though neither could move.

Cam cleared his throat and looked away first. She continued to observe him. She guessed him to be about thirty. He was tanned as though he worked outside, and there were a couple of small scars on the side of his face. She was wondering about them when the car came to a halt in front of the restaurant.

"I'll get the door, Donavan, thanks. Pick us up in about an hour and fifteen minutes," Cam instructed the driver as he exited the car and helped Chris to her feet.

The restaurant certainly lived up to what she had heard about it. A uniformed doorman opened the door with a deep bow to them. The maître d' greeted them cordially, and they were immediately led to a secluded table. A waiter appeared with menus as soon as they were seated.

"Good evening, sir. It's a pleasure having you here again. Would you like a drink before dinner?" he asked as he opened the menus and placed them on the table.

"How are you, James? It's always nice to come here," Cam acknowledged the young man.

"Would you like a drink?" Cam turned his attention back to his companion.

"I—don't know. I'm not very good at this sort of thing. Perhaps you could suggest something mild. If you are going to have something, that is," Chris stammered.

Too late, Cam realized he had overestimated her experience. If he didn't do something, her whole evening could be ruined, and that was the last thing he wanted!

"I'll tell you what. Put yourself in my hands for this evening. I'll make all the decisions, and all you have to do is enjoy yourself. How would that be?" He held his breath, waiting for an answer.

"That would be just fine with me." Chris smiled weakly. Somehow Cam seemed to have a knack for making her feel safe. As if nothing could harm her as long as he was near.

"We are a little short on time, James. I think we will order now."

"Very good, sir." James bowed slightly.

"We'll start with a house salad and Italian dressing. Next we will have grilled chicken breast with wild rice and mushrooms, along with mixed steamed vegetables." He turned to Chris. "Does that sound all right for you?"

"It sounds perfect," she answered. "I guess I'm hungrier than I thought because suddenly I'm famished." She finished with a grin because for some reason she didn't quite understand, all at once she felt very lighthearted. This had all the signs of becoming a night she would remember forever. For this one night, she really was Cinderella in a beautiful gown, on the arm of Prince Charming. Just for this one night, the reality of tomorrow didn't exist.

While they waited on the food, Chris let her eyes wander about the room, trying to commit it to memory for future daydreams. Her view was partially blocked by lush greenery on either side of their table, but there was little doubt of the plush surroundings. Each table had a small chandelier of what appeared to be sterling silver, entwined with delicate greenery and rosebuds suspended immediately above it. Those were the only lights visible. Indirect lighting was skillfully concealed behind ivory wall panels to provide just the correct amount of illumination for the diners. Mauve, blue, and cream tablecloths gave subtle color to the décor; and strategically placed greenery, in the form of small trees and hanging baskets, provided seclusion for the patrons. Thick beige carpeting silenced the footsteps of the staff as they moved quietly among the occupied tables.

While Chris studied her surroundings, Cam watched her. From what little he knew about her, he was sure she carried too many responsibilities for someone her age. He still wasn't prepared to admit it, even to himself, but this girl and her little family were going to have a profound effect on his life. He had yet to find a way to help her, but in order to do that he first had to find a way to keep her in his life.

"Have you always lived here in Everett?" Cam's voice brought Chris back to the table.

"Yes. Actually, I have always lived in the same house. My parents built it before I was born. My dad fenced in the back yard so we would have a safe place to play. He always said he was going to entertain his grandchildren there in due time."

"You speak of your dad in the past tense. What happened?" he asked quietly.

Ramona had related the conversation she had with Chris earlier, but he needed for her to tell him so she wouldn't think they had been discussing her behind her back.

"A plane crash killed both my parents. Three years ago," she answered his question.

"I'm sorry. It must have been rough. What were you—fifteen?"

"I was sixteen and ready to start my senior year in high school. Luci, my sister, had graduated the year before, and the twins were three. Luci was eighteen, so the courts let us stay together. A social worker kept her eye on us for a couple of years until I turned eighteen. I guess she must have decided every thing was all right because she quit coming around. Money from their estate allowed us to keep the house. I couldn't afford daycare for the twins, so I didn't go back for my senior year. As soon as I could, I went to night school and got my diploma. Luci mostly watched the kids while I was in school, and when she couldn't, we had a very nice neighbor who would care for them." She didn't know why she gave him all that information. Perhaps because he was so easy to talk to.

She was relieved when their salads came. For the next few minutes they busied themselves with their meal.

Before Cam could ask any more questions, Chris changed the subject. She was curious about her companion. The only thing she knew about him was his name and where he lived, although she wasn't sure she could find his house even though she had been there twice.

"I don't believe I've heard you say what you do for a living. What sort of business are you involved in?" Curiosity made her ask the question.

"I'm half owner in a computer chip design firm," he answered after a short pause.

"It must be very successful," Chris ventured.

"Do you mean, am I wealthy?" he answered tersely.

"Oh no, that's not what I meant at all!" Chris sputtered. Embarrassed that Cam would think that she was interested in his money. "It's just that—well you strike me as being a very self-assured person. I can't see you failing at any task you set your mind to do."

He was relieved at the explanation she gave him. He would have bet his life that money wasn't the driving force for Chris. "Well, I've had my ups and downs. I owe a great deal of my success to a man named Peter Kelso. We were college roommates. I come up with the ideas, and Pete has the brains to carry them out. We seem to make a pretty fair team."

Their conversation was once again interrupted by the arrival of food. The main course was everything Chris expected. The chicken breast and vegetables tasted as good as they looked, and she had no trouble eating it all. It had been a long time since she had eaten restaurant food, and never any that tasted better.

Cam noticed her obvious enjoyment and made a mental note to take her to dinner again in the near future.

"Are you ready for dessert?" he asked after she had emptied her plate.

Chris looked up to see a dessert cart full of everything from cakes and pies to puddings and gelatin treats. She couldn't begin to decide which she wanted.

Cam couldn't help but smile as he watched her expressions as she tried to choose. She reminded him of a child in a candy store trying to pick out one piece of candy.

"If you can't select one, Chris, why don't you have a little taste of several? I'm sure James will be glad to prepare you a plate."

"Oh! Could I do that?" She breathed a sigh of relief and looked at James, who nodded in agreement, then immediately picked out three of her absolute favorites.

"I hope you don't think me greedy." She felt embarrassed when she realized she was actually having three desserts while Cam was only having one, a piece of chocolate cheesecake.

"Of course not! Actually I'm pleased to see you enjoying your food. Too many people this day and age spend so much time worrying about their weight or some such thing that they don't know how to appreciate good food." He wished they could stay a little longer, but it was nearly time for them to go. As soon as she finished eating, he signed the check so they could be on their way.

Donavan was waiting at the curb to whisk them to the theater. Chris had passed by it many times, but she had never been inside. She found it to be even grander than she expected.

She was unaware of the envious eyes following them as they made their way across the lobby. She had no idea what a striking couple they were, he in his tuxedo and she in her brilliant blue gown. She hadn't realized just how nervous she would be when they finally arrived at the theater. She clutched his arm in an effort to steady herself until they reached their seats.

This was the first live musical she had ever attended, and it held her spellbound. She laughed and cried along with the actors. When the final curtain went down, she felt emotionally drained. Somehow, Cam's handkerchief had found its way into her hand, and she had used it several times to wipe away tears, sometimes from laughter and sometimes from sadness.

"I'm sorry about this," she apologized as she returned it to him. "It seems you are always coming to my rescue."

"A role I find quite acceptable," he replied as they rose to make their way out of the theater.

Once again, Donavan was waiting for them. Cam assisted her into the car and sat quietly beside her, allowing her time to collect her thoughts before their next stop.

She noticed the pain was back. It must have been the excitement of the evening that that caused it. She would feel better after a good night's sleep in her own bed. The car glided to a halt in front of Cam's house instead of hers.

"I would really rather go home if you don't mind," she objected.

"I thought you might sleep better if we stopped here first so you can check on the kids to be sure they are okay," he explained.

"Yes, that is a good idea. They haven't ever stayed away from home overnight, before. I will just run up and look in on them. It won't take long."

The children were sleeping peacefully, and when she returned downstairs, she found Cam fixing hot chocolate for them to drink.

"I thought we might have something to drink before we call it an evening." For some reason he couldn't explain, he wanted to prolong their time together.

"Hot chocolate does sound good. Perhaps one cup won't hurt, and then I really have to go." She didn't feel well at all, but she also wanted the evening to last just a little while longer. After sitting for a few minutes, she didn't seem to have the energy to get up. She wondered briefly if Cam had put something in the drink.

"Since it's so late, why don't you spend the night here? I'm sure your things are still in the same room. I can take you home in the morning." Cam noticed her eyes drooping.

"No really, I want to go home tonight. You can bring my things when you return the kids' clothes if you don't mind, that is."

She summoned the strength to get to her feet, and then everything went black and she, once again, fell limply into Cam's waiting arms.

The next thing she was aware of was Ramona placing a cool damp cloth on her forehead. She was lying on a bed and in terrible pain. She heard a faint voice say the doctor would be right over.

"I don't need a doctor. I've just overdone it tonight. Let me rest tonight, and I'm sure I will be all right tomorrow."

"You do need to see a doctor and that's why I called him!" The tone of Cam's voice stilled any further argument she might have had.

After a brief examination, the doctor determined that surgery was called for. He told them Chris had appendicitis, and he thought it was on the verge of rupturing. He gave her something for the pain and asked to use their phone to call an ambulance.

"I'll take her." Cam moved into action. "It will be faster." He turned to Ramona. "If you will, go down and tell Donavan what we are going to do, and I will bring her right down."

Chris was very still and pale when he bent over to pick her up. It had been a real struggle for him to carry her up the stairs before, but this time he was so concerned for her that he didn't even notice the pain as he retraced his steps.

She had only a vague memory of being carried and then riding in a car. She remembered someone in a white coat telling her that she needed an operation. She was too weak to object, and when someone handed her a paper to sign, she looked at Cam to see what to do. He told her it would be all right, and she needed to sign her name. Someone gave her another shot, and the last thing she remembered was being rolled into a room with bright lights and someone telling her to relax and breathe deeply.

When next she woke, the first thing she noticed, with relief, was that the pain was gone. Slowly she looked around, trying to figure out where she was. The first thing to catch her eye was the largest bouquet of flowers she had ever seen. The sun was shining on them, so she knew it was at least morning.

Just then the door opened slightly, and Kathleen peeked in. When she saw Chris was awake, she entered the room and approached the bed.

"Hi! I'm glad you're awake. How do you feel?" She reached out and picked up Chris's hand, holding it gently.

"I don't know yet. I don't hurt anymore, and I'm really thirsty, but I guess I'm all right." She was having trouble thinking straight. "Where are Jon and Jenny? Tell them not to worry about me. I'll call my sister to come home and take care of them." Surely Luci would come home now that they really needed her.

"The kids are fine. Cam was here all night. He left here a few minutes ago to take them to school. My mother told them what happened and promised they could come see you this afternoon after school. She said that seemed to satisfy them. I brought some things for you. Mother said you left rather suddenly last night. I gathered you weren't in any shape to bring anything with you. So you can tell me what else you want." Kathleen patted her hand.

"Could you find my purse? I don't remember if I brought it with me or not. It might still be in the car. I'm so sorry to be so much trouble to you. I'll never forget the things your family has done for us. I don't know how I can ever repay you," Chris apologized, near tears.

"Now Chris! We'll have none of that! We are just glad to have been here when you needed help. Don't worry about anything but getting well. Now that is an order! Okay?" Kathleen squeezed her hand and frowned in mock anger at her.

Just then the door opened again, and Cam entered the room.

"I see you have another visitor, so I will leave you." Kathleen moved out of the way so Cam could approach the bed. "I'll be back this afternoon."

"I must say, you are looking better," Cam ventured as he studied her face.

"I'm feeling better." She was embarrassed to have Cam peering so intently at her. She must look like a mess.

"Do you know who sent the flowers?" She asked in an attempt to get him to stop looking at her.

"I had them delivered. I didn't know what kind of flowers you liked, so I asked the shop to send some of every kind they had," Cam admitted, a trifle sheepishly. "No one should ever be in a hospital without flowers," he added. "I saw this in your bedroom at Ramona's this morning when I picked the kids up for school. Thought you might need it." He laid her purse on the table beside her bed.

"Thank you." Chris paused, and then continued, "It seems I've caused you nothing but trouble in the two days you have known me. I'm so sorry."

"Well, I will admit, you have given me a couple of bad moments. You seem so alone in the world and so young to have the responsibilities you apparently have. I think it's high time someone stepped in and gave you a hand. I'm just happy to have been there to catch you. Both times." Cam bent down and gave Chris a very tender kiss on the forehead.

She had almost forgotten what it felt like to have someone to take care of her. Someone who made her feel safe and secure. This was a man she knew she could truly rely on. Of that, she had no doubt. Her throat was so full she couldn't speak. A single tear found its way down her cheek.

"Here! I'll have none of that!" he admonished her as he very carefully wiped the tear away with his finger. "I'm going to leave you to rest for a while. I'll try to bring the kids by this afternoon. If I can't get away, Kathleen will bring them."

When the nurse came in, Chris asked if she could use the phone. She had slipped Luci's phone number in her purse before she left home. She hoped Luci would answer, but a man's voice came on the phone.

"Is Luci Walker there, please?"

"Yeah, she's probably around somewhere. Wait a minute."

After what seemed like an eternity, Luci picked up the phone.

"Hello."

"Luci, it's Chris."

"Hi. Did you get my stuff sent?"

"I'm sorry but I haven't yet. You see—"

"Why not? I need my things now. Hurry up and send them."

"I can't. That's why I'm calling. I'm in the hospital because I had to have my appendix removed last night. Luci, I need you to come home to take care of Jon and Jenny, at least until I'm up and around again."

"How can you ask me to come home now? You know this could be my big chance!" Luci was not happy. "Where are the kids now?"

"They are with friends for now, but I can't—," Chris started to explain.

"Can't they just stay where they are for a few days longer? They're big enough to help you once you get home. You don't really need me, do you?" Luci finished quickly. "I have to go now. Frank's waiting. I will make do for a few more days, but send my stuff as soon as you can. Bye."

The phone went dead before Chris could say another word. She felt utterly defeated. What was she going to do now? She turned onto her side, curled up, and cried herself to sleep.

"It's time for lunch." The nurse was patting her on the shoulder. "Are you having pain?" She asked when she noticed the swollen eyes and tear stained face.

"No, I'm feeling pretty good. I'm afraid that I'm not very hungry though." She tried to smile as she turned over so the tray could be placed in front of her.

"I'm afraid that you don't get very much right now, but you need to try to eat something. After lunch we will try sitting up for a few minutes while I make up your bed. Okay?"

The nurse busied herself arranging the lunch tray so Chris could reach everything.

"There. I won't be far away if you need something."

Her first meal was mostly liquid, but she found it to be very tasty, and to her surprise, it was soon all gone.

With a little help from the nurse she made it to a nearby chair, but she was quite ready to return to the bed as soon as it was ready for her. She fell asleep instantly.

Kathleen and Ramona stopped by to see her. They tiptoed into the room and stood quietly looking at the sleeping girl.

"Let's let her sleep. The poor child is probably just worn out. She is so young to have so much on her plate. We'll come back later." Ramona's sympathetic words were echoed by Kathleen's thoughts as they silently left the room after laying a robe and gown on the foot of her bed.

They were the first things she saw when she woke up. She rang the nurse to ask if she would help her put them on and then let her sit up again for a while.

Cam brought the twins by a few minutes later. She was glad to be up when they got there.

She opened her arms to welcome the worried children. It was the first time since their parents' death that the three of them had been apart overnight, and she couldn't believe how much she missed them.

"Remember what I told you, kids. Chris has a really sore stomach!" Cam's voice slowed their headlong rush to greet their sister. Carefully they approached Chris, stopping before they touched her.

"My tummy may be sore, but there is nothing wrong with my arms, so come give me a hug. Just be careful." Fear turned to happiness when once again they were secure in the arms of their big sister.

"I really missed you. Are you all right?" Jon was the first one to pull away.

"I'm much better now that you are here. I'm sorry I had to leave without telling you. I hope you didn't worry too much." She gave Jenny another squeeze before letting her move away.

"When can we go home?" Jenny finally found her tongue. "Is Luci coming home to take care of us while you are sick?"

"No, honey. She's not. I talked to her a little ago, and she said that she was sorry but she just couldn't get away right now." Chris smiled as she answered, trying not to worry the little girl.

"But who is going to take care of us while you are here?" Jon was starting to feel a little uneasy.

"Don't worry. We'll think of something." Chris winked at Jon. "Haven't we always managed?"

Cam, having quietly sat by watching the reunion, broke in. "How would you kids like to stay with me for a few days? Maybe your sister will let us go by your house and pick up some things you will need. I'll take you to school in the mornings, and then you can come by here every afternoon to see Chris. Do you think that would be okay?"

"I'm sorry, Chris, I should have asked you first, but I don't want the kids to get upset," he apologized.

"I feel like I'm taking advantage of you, but I don't know what else to do. It won't be for long, and then I promise we will stop imposing on your hospitality." Once again, Cam had stepped in to solve her problems, and she could only feel relief. What would they have done if he hadn't been there?

"Believe me when I say we don't mind at all. Besides, I think it will do Ramona good to have the kids there. I'm sure sometimes she feels as though no one needs her since my father's death, so this will give her a new focus in her life." Cam tried to relieve some of the worry and frustration that he knew Chris must be feeling along about now.

Where was that sister? What could she possibly have to do that was more important than her family? He would love to ask Chris these questions and more, but he held his tongue. He couldn't think of anything that could be more important than family. He promised himself that he would have some answers before he let Chris and the twins out of his life. He had a gut feeling though that no matter how many answers he got, he would always want more from her.

"Well, she is up already! I must say you look much better than I expected." Kathleen entered the room with Ramona right behind her, holding a small bouquet of roses from her garden. She set the flowers on the table by the bed and bent to give Chris a light peck on the cheek.

"They are lovely. You are all being too kind to me." It had been a long time since anyone showed this much concern for her.

"I'm glad you came by." Cam stepped in to give Chris a chance to compose herself. "I've taken the liberty of inviting Jon and Jenny to stay with us while Chris is here."

"That's wonderful! It will be a pleasure to have them. Chris, I insist that you join them until you are completely well." Ramona squeezed Chris's hand then turned to the twins. "Children, when I left, I think Ellen was getting ready to make some oatmeal cookies. How does that sound to you?"

"Great! That's our favorite!" Jon could hardly wait to taste them.

"I don't think there is a cookie made that is not their favorite." Chris laughed, feeling happier by the minute. Her siblings were going to be well cared for, and she was not going to have worry about how she was going to manage while she recuperated. She would worry about tomorrow later.

"Well, it sounds like you two have cookies waiting for you." Cam rose from his seat, preparing to leave. "Chris, if you will give me your house key, we will go by and pick up what the kids need, and then hit the cookies before they get cold."

Chris retrieved the keys from her purse and handed them to Cam.

"Hey, you two! How about giving me another hug before you leave?"

"All right, but I think we had better hurry. I'm getting hungry for a cookie!" Jon gave Chris a brief hug. Jenny's was a little longer because she was torn between the cookies and leaving Chris.

The cookies won, and she joined Jon in taking Cam's hand trying to hurry him along through the door.

"I don't think you need to worry about the kids." He laughed as he allowed the eager children to pull him toward the door. "I think you should feel sorry for me trying to keep up with them. They're going to be just fine. We'll take good care of them, I promise."

The next few days at the hospital passed quickly for Chris. The food was good, and she had no trouble eating every bite. When she had no company, she slept.

Every afternoon, Kathleen brought the children by to see her. They seemed to be adapting well to their temporary home. She was sure that Ellen was spoiling them because every day they were in a hurry to get home to see what she was making for them to sample.

Cam stopped by every day, usually at noon while she was eating. If he was busy then, he came when he could. He always brought ice cream or candy or something for her to read.

"Well, I think you can go home tomorrow, Chris." The doctor smiled at her as he sat on the foot of her bed.

"Thank you, Doctor Lash, it will be good to get home." Chris paused, and then continued, "Doctor—about my bill. I'll have to pay you a little at a time, but I promise I will pay you everything I owe you."

"Don't worry about that. Your bill has already been taken care of." Doctor Lash sought to ease her concerns.

"Paid? But how? By whom?" She knew there had to be a mistake.

"I don't know. My office manager handles those matters. I'll notify the front desk that you will be leaving in the morning. I would like to see you in my office in two weeks." With that, he got up to leave the room.

"You have been very kind, Doctor. I appreciate everything that you have done for me," Chris voiced her thanks to the gentle man standing beside the bed.

"It's been my pleasure. Don't forget. Two weeks." With that, he left.

"Hi." Cam arrived just as she was finishing her lunch.

"Hello. Guess what? I get to go home tomorrow." She couldn't wait to tell someone, and he was her first visitor.

"That's great news. Did he say what time?"

"In the morning. Doctor Lash said his bill has already been paid. That has to be a mistake, so I told him I would pay him as soon as I can. I'll do the same with my hospital charges. I guess I will give up my classes at school and look for a full time job as soon as I can. I asked the nurse to bring me a copy of my hospital bill, but she hasn't yet."

"That wasn't a mistake with Doctor Lash's bill, and all of the charges here are being taken care of also." Cam took a deep breath and continued his explanation, praying she wouldn't be too upset with him. "I didn't want you to have to worry about money right now, so I took care of everything."

Chris was stunned. After a moment she responded. "I appreciate what you have done for me, but the bills are still mine to pay. The only difference is, now I am indebted to you instead of Doctor Lash and the hospital. Could you please give me a copy of all the charges?"

"That's not necessary. I did it because I wanted to, certainly not to make you obligated to me. Let's just forget the whole thing," Cam tried, again, to explain his actions.

"I'm sorry, but I can't do that. I've always paid my debts, and I don't intend to start taking charity now. Somehow, I will repay you. No matter how long it takes, I will see that everything is repaid."

"Okay, okay! If it's that important to you, we'll work something out." He knew she had dug in her heels, and for the first time in a long while, he was about to lose an argument.

"Promise?"

"Promise and cross my heart." He solemnly crossed his hand over his chest.

"I'll pay the going interest also?" Chris tried not to grin at his motion.

"Don't push it, lady, or you will pay double interest." Cam detected the grin she had tried to cover, and a feeling of relief swept through his body as he grinned openly back at her.

"Will you give me copies of everything you pay and have already paid?"

"Yes, yes. Anything you want!" Cam surrendered. "Now am I forgiven?"

"Yes, I forgive you." She reached out to shake hands on the agreement, but instead he captured her hand, turned it over, and very gently kissed the back of it.

The touch of his lips to her skin started a tingle that invaded every part of her body. She had seen it done many times in the movies and read about it in books, but never had she come close to imagining the electric feeling it created when it actually happened.

"Well, what do we have here?" Kathleen fairly beamed when she saw what was taking place as she opened the door.

Chris jerked her hand back, embarrassed to have Kathleen get the wrong idea.

"Our young lady is being dismissed in the morning." Cam smoothly changed the subject.

"Wonderful!" Kathleen took the hint. "I expect you will be glad to leave here, won't you? Let me know when you are ready so I can pick you up and take you to Mother's. The children are going to be tickled."

"Are you sure she won't mind me staying there for a few days?"

"Of course she doesn't mind. I think she will be a little sad when it comes time for Jon and Jenny to leave. So will Ellen, but I doubt that she will admit it. She lets the children have free run of her kitchen whenever they want. Mother and I are frowned at if we do any more than walk through it," Kathleen answered with a chuckle.

"We're all quite taken with the kids. It's easy to understand because they are very remarkable children," Cam added as he got up. "I guess I better get back to work. I'll bring the kids by this afternoon. In the meantime, you take a nap."

"I'll go along too," Kathleen said after Cam had gone. "If you would like, I will go by your house and pick up a few things for you. I can bring something in for you to wear home tomorrow. I bet you are tired of wearing gowns by now."

"It would be nice to have clothes on. I would appreciate it if you would look around to see if everything is okay. You know, see if the refrigerator and deep freeze are running, and just look around." She handed the house key to Kathleen.

"Certainly, I'll check everything. I think Cam shut off the water when he picked up the kids' things." With that Kathleen left, suggesting Chris take a nap before school was out.

"Is she going to sleep all the time we're here?" Jon's voice roused Chris.

She opened her eyes to find three pairs of eyes peering at her.

"Hi, kids. Cam. My goodness, I didn't realize it was that late. How was school today?" She smothered a yawn as she tried to wake up.

"It was fine." Jenny moved as close to the bed as she could get. She for one would be very glad when she could climb up on her big sister's lap any time she wanted to, like it used to be. "I played with Sarah at recess, and Miss James let us draw a picture today. I will show it to you as soon as I can bring it home."

"How did your day go, Jon?"

"It was okay." He wasn't as fond of school as his sister. He would rather talk to Cam about his cars.

"Did Cam tell you I get to go home tomorrow?" she asked.

"Really? Oh boy! I'm sure glad," Jenny cheered.

"Are we going back to our house?" Jon asked.

"Not right now. We'll stay at Ramona's for a few days until I get a little stronger, then we'll go home. Is that all right with you?" She always liked to include the twins in any major decisions she made.

"We won't mind at all, will we, Jen?"

"No, we like it there. Ramona helps us with our homework, and Ellen lets us have cookies and things when we get home from school," Jenny replied. "And, Chris, would you care if we called Ramona grandma, like Bobby and Sarah do? We asked her, and she said she wouldn't mind, but we had to ask you first."

"Since we don't have a grandma of our own, Bobby said we could share his if we wanted to," Jon added.

"Grandma? I don't know." Chris searched for words. When she got well and they returned to their little house, she doubted their paths would cross very often, and she didn't want the children to become too attached to Ramona and her family.

"I think it's time for you kids to go home now," Cam, sensing her indecision, cut into the conversation. "You can discuss this later. Right now, I think we should let Chris get back to her nap. Besides, I have to get back to work."

Cam bent over and winked at Jon. "If it helps any, I think it's a great idea."

"Did you hear that, Chris? Cam thinks it's a great idea!"

"I heard. But that doesn't mean you can. We will talk about it later." She shot a sharp look at Cam, wishing fervently he had kept quiet.

She tried to glare at Cam, but she couldn't keep from laughing as he grinned and winked at her as they ducked out the door. She knew that they felt like they had won the first round, but she wasn't through yet. She had some serious thinking to do before they talked on the subject again.

Kathleen appeared promptly at nine the next morning. By nine thirty, Chris was dressed and waiting for the nurse to take her downstairs to the car waiting to take her to Ramona's.

"Well, here we are. Are you ready? Do you have everything?" The nurse came bustling into the room pushing a wheelchair.

"I don't need that. I can walk to the car. It's not very far and I feel fine." Chris eyed the chair.

"I know you are fine, but its hospital policy, so if you have everything, hop aboard." The nurse was firm.

Chris conceded and sat in the chair without another word.

"You have been a delight as a patient," The nurse complimented Chris as she pushed her down the hall. "We are all going to miss you."

"Thank you, you have all been very nice, and I appreciate everything you have done for me," Chris thanked the nurse as she delivered her to the waiting car.

Chapter Five

A huge banner greeted Chris as she opened the front door. "WELCOME HOME CHRIS" was written in crayon, and small flowers were drawn around the edges. At least she thought they were flowers.

Chris was so surprised she couldn't utter a word.

"They were working on it when I left to pick you up." Kathleen laughed as she filled in the silence. "I'm not sure whose idea it was, but when I left, Mother and Ellen were crawling around on the floor, trying to get it lettered so the kids could get the coloring done before you got here."

"It's a good thing it's Saturday because I don't think we could have pried the kids out of the house to go to school." Kathleen gently prodded Chris from the spot she seemed frozen to.

"Do you like our surprise?" Jon and Jenny had been waiting anxiously for Chris to see their handiwork.

"Oh yes, children. It's a wonderful surprise, and I will keep it forever." It felt really good to be home, well almost home, Chris thought as she hugged the twins tightly.

"We're all very happy you are here, aren't we children?" Ramona came forward to greet Chris.

"We're really glad you are here too," Bobby and Sarah shyly approached Chris.

"Thank you all, it's certainly wonderful to be out of the hospital."

"Kathleen, why don't you help Chris upstairs so she can get a little rest before lunch? I'm sure she's tired," Ramona suggested.

After setting the suitcase on a chair, Kathleen opened the window so fresh air could enter the room.

"Take a nap if you wish. I'll come up and see you later." With that she withdrew so Chris could rest.

Chris stood for a moment, looking around the room. It was such a pleasant space that she couldn't help but feel a small pang of regret that she would soon be leaving it.

Her own house was quite comfortable, and she would be happy to return there. But there, she would be in the real world with her real problems. Here, at least for a little while, she could let someone take care of her.

From what she could see, the children were content, so maybe she should rest and enjoy herself for a couple of days. She hated taking advantage of Ramona's hospitality, but it would be nice to get some strength back before she took over the running of her own house once again.

Quickly, she changed into a night gown and slipped into the welcoming bed.

"Chris, are you awake?" She opened her eyes to find Jon and Jenny watching her. When they saw her eyes open, they crawled onto the bed, one on each side of her.

"Is your tummy still sore?" Jenny asked before she got too close to her.

"It's well enough for me to hold you two little monkeys." She put her arms around both of the children and pulled them close.

"I'm awfully glad you are out of the hospital," Jenny spoke first.

"We missed you something awful," Jon added. "Everybody has been good to us, but it wasn't like having you here with us."

"I'm glad to be here too. I hope we can go home in a few days so we can get back to normal." Chris gave them an extra hug. "Would you like that?"

"Yeah, except that we will miss Ellen. She's really neat, and she makes good cookies. She tells us funny stories sometimes," Jon said thoughtfully.

"Cam reads us a story every night before he tucks us in. I guess we will sort of miss that too," Jenny added softly.

"So this is where you disappeared to." Kathleen stuck her head through the partially open door. "Lunch is ready, kids. Chris, I will bring you a tray in a few minutes."

"Please don't go to any bother, I can come down for lunch." She didn't want to cause anymore trouble to this family than she already had.

"It's no trouble at all. Besides, Cam would skin us alive if we made you walk downstairs on your first day here," Kathleen brushed aside her objections.

Chris spent most of the afternoon sitting by the window. The fresh air felt good to her. Jenny spent a good bit of the time with her, chatting about things that had happened in the last few days. Jon kept them company for a little while, and then he went in search of Ellen to see what she was doing.

She knew she should have gotten dressed, but she was so comfortable. She would dress before she went down for the evening meal.

"Are you decent?" Cam asked as he rapped sharply on the door of the room that was a temporary home for Chris.

"Come in," Jenny answered before Chris could say a word. She pulled her robe closely around her neck as Cam entered the room. She had become used to him seeing her in a robe at the hospital, but somehow it was different in the privacy of her bedroom.

The motion did not go unnoticed as he crossed the room, taking a seat across from her.

"How are you feeling?" he asked, peering at her face.

"Pretty good. I've been sitting here all afternoon enjoying the heavenly fresh air."

"I've been here with her all afternoon too," Jenny chimed in, grinning from ear to ear.

She was so glad to once again be able to spend time alone with her big sister. She liked everyone there, but there was no one that could take the place of Chris.

"That's great!" he answered. "You see, kids, I told you that Chris would be well and home soon, didn't I?" He turned to Jenny, and then Jon, who had followed him up the stairs.

"Yes you did, but we still worried a little," Jon admitted.

"Well, that's behind us now. How would you feel about a cookout tonight? I think Ellen and Donavan are fixing all kinds of food as we speak. How about it? Does anyone want to go help?"

"Oh boy!" Jon jumped up from his perch on the bed. "Come on, Jen, let's go see what we can do. We'll see you later, Chris."

After the twins left, Cam sat for a moment, studying their temporary houseguest.

He doubted if she had any idea just how fragile or how lovely she looked, sitting there with her robe tucked tightly under her chin.

"Jenny was a little frightened when we told her where you were. I think she was a little afraid you wouldn't come back," Cam admitted.

"I'm not really surprised at that. Jon had always been the more independent of the two. Neither of them really remembers our parents, but they know that they left on a trip and never came back. I think she has always been a little afraid that I might do the same thing."

"What about your older sister?" Cam had refrained from asking about Luci so far, but curiosity made him ask now.

"She was usually working. I have always spent more time with them than she has. I think sometimes they forget that I'm their sister and think of me as their mother," Chris tried to explain.

"That's a lot of responsibility for someone your age," Cam commented thoughtfully.

"Oh I don't mind," Chris hastened to add. "I'm just glad I could be there for them when they needed someone."

"Well, you have done a fine job with them. I've never seen better mannered children, including my niece and nephew." Cam stood to leave. "I'll bring a tray up in a little bit. Would you prefer hotdog or hamburger?"

"Actually, I like both, but I can go downstairs for dinner." Chris carefully rose from her chair to show him she was okay. "If you will give me a few minutes to freshen up and get dressed, I will be right down."

"I won't hear of it!" Cam stopped her. "I don't want you to do anything for a couple of days. Then we can discuss your activities."

"If you insist." She sighed dramatically. It felt so good to be pampered, if only for a little while.

"I do." Cam frowned in mock anger. "Now you lie down for a while, and I will be up soon with your food."

"Okay, sleepyhead, wake up." Her short rest had turned into a nap. She opened her eyes to see Cam standing at the foot of her bed, holding a tray loaded with food. He busied himself spreading their food on the table by the window, while Chris freshened herself up.

"My gosh! That's enough for six people!" Chris exclaimed when she saw the table filled to overflowing with food.

"I wanted to be sure we had enough," Cam answered as he handed her a plate. "Dig in. I don't know about you, but I'm starving."

"I wasn't very hungry until I saw all this food. Now I'm famished."

Once again, Cam proved to be an entertaining dinner companion. After a few minutes, she lost her apprehension of having him share her meal in her bedroom.

The two days Chris had planned to stay turned into a week. Each morning, Cam insisted on having breakfast with her. Every day, promptly at six thirty, he knocked on her door with a tray loaded with breakfast for two.

After the first two days, he allowed her to go downstairs for her other meals, but he remained adamant about breakfast. He also visited her room every evening to check on her progress, he said.

At first, she found it a little uncomfortable to have Cam in the room while she was in bed, but gradually she grew accustomed to his presence. Soon she found herself looking forward to his visits, even though some nights he was so late that she found herself hard put to stay awake until he showed up. But stay awake she did!

Without realizing it, little by little she was telling him all about her life and her family, with her parents before their deaths, and with her siblings afterward. She told him of her dreams for the future, not that she expected them to come to fruition any time soon now. The one subject she found she couldn't discuss was Luci. For some reason she wasn't ready to admit, even to herself, that Luci was too self-absorbed to be of any real help as far as family matters were concerned.

One morning as she made her way downstairs, she heard a strange voice. As she entered the sitting room, a man she hadn't seen before rose from his place on the sofa beside Ramona and came forward to greet her.

He was, without a doubt, one of the most handsome men she had ever seen! His blond hair had been artfully styled to lie in waves down on his collar. A narrow mustache had been trimmed to a perfect arch over thin lips. She felt certain that his limpid blue eyes were boring into her very soul.

"So this is the little invalid I've been hearing so much about." He lifted her hand to kiss the back of it. She couldn't explain why, but the action made her want to shiver.

"Chris, this is my son, Scott Windsor," Ramona's words interrupted her thoughts. "He's been away on vacation." She moved to place her hand on her son's arm.

"Does Cam know you're back?" Kathleen asked as she arrived on the scene.

"Not yet," Scott answered with a laugh.

"Somehow, I don't think he's going to be too happy to see you." Kathleen shook her head as she took a seat.

"Nonsense! This is your home, Scott. Of course he will be glad to have you here," Ramona protested.

"Let's go out on the terrace." Scott took Chris's arm and led her to a seat near the pool.

After a few minutes of desultory conversation, Scott sprang to his feet and began pacing back and forth along the edge of the pool.

"How would you feel about going for a ride?" he asked. "It's too nice of a day to be stuck here."

"It is a pretty day." She hesitated. "I don't suppose anyone would mind if I went out for a while. I haven't been anywhere since I got here." Suddenly she couldn't wait to go.

In a matter of minutes, she was seated beside Scott in a little red sports car.

She regretted her decision before they had traveled very far. Scott drove too fast and frequently passed cars carelessly, often taking his eyes off the road to look at her. Chris was on the verge of asking him to take her home when he slammed on the brakes and turned off onto a narrow winding road, which led to a clearing at the top of a bluff.

Without saying a word, Scott stopped the car, leaped out, strode to the edge of the clearing and stood facing the valley below.

After a few moments, Chris joined him to see what he was looking at with such intensity.

She was mildly surprised to see the Eastland factory directly below where they were standing.

"All of that was supposed to be mine. The old man told me he wanted me to take over when he retired. After he died, I did run it for a while, but then as soon as Cam could, he came and took it away from me." The bitterness in Scott's voice peaked Chris's curiosity.

"But isn't your name Windsor? I thought the Eastland family owned the company." Chris was confused.

"Cam's father owned it. He was my stepfather. He and my mother were married ten years ago. Cam is my stepbrother, and Kathleen is my sister. She was seventeen, and I was fourteen when we moved here."

When he turned to face her, the bitterness in Scott's eyes startled her.

"But Cam's last name is Cameron. I don't understand." Chris couldn't figure out what he was talking about.

"Of course you don't. He probably swore everyone to secrecy to be sure they didn't tell you the truth, but I will be happy to fill you in. His real name is Phillip Cameron Eastland the Second. Mother told me you used to work at the factory. He is directly responsible for the loss of your job. It was his decision to cut back on the work force. You are only here because he feels sorry for you. If he really wanted to help, he would give control of the factory back to me so I could rehire everybody he had laid off," Scott happily supplied her with the information.

A sharp stab of pain shot through her as she listened to Scott's words.

They had been lying to her all along! All of them were in on it! She trusted them! There was only one thing she could do now.

"Will you take me ho—to Ramona's now?" She had to pack up and get away from there as soon as she could.

"What are you going to do?"

"I'm going back to my own house. I would appreciate it if you would drive us there as soon as I get our things together."

She learned that Ramona had taken the children to a movie, so that would give her time to pack everything and be ready to leave as soon as they got back. She had the twins' things gathered up in no time and was packing up her belongings when a knock on the door interrupted her thoughts. She expected it was Scott, so without pausing she called for him to come in. Kathleen stepped into the room and stood speechless as she looked at the disheveled state of the room.

"What are you doing?" She finally gasped.

"Now that I know the real reason I'm here, I'm going home where I belong." She barely glanced up from her task at hand.

"But how did you—why do you think you are here?" Kathleen had come to ask a favor. This was the last thing she expected.

"Scott told me the whole story." Chris stood, hands on hips, facing a stunned Kathleen.

"It's Cam's fault that I lost my job! It's Cam's fault that I will have to drop out of school! It's Cam's fault that I will probably never get the chance to ever become a professional anything!" Chris counted each of Cam's sins. "In fact if it weren't for him, I would be home, and just maybe, by now I would have had a job so I could have begun to put my life back together!" She knew that she had to stay angry because that was the only thing keeping the tears at bay. There would be plenty of time for them later.

"But, Chris." Kathleen hesitated, not quite sure how to proceed. "Please, you can't just leave! Won't you stop and listen to me for just a minute? I came here today because I am really in need of your help!"

"You need my help? How could you possibly need me for anything? The only reason I'm here is because Cam—excuse me—Mr. Eastland felt sorry for me," Chris interjected. "Look around you. What on earth could you possibly need that you can't get for yourself if you really wanted it?"

"First, I want to say this." Kathleen took a deep breath before she began. She understood the anger that Chris was feeling. She didn't doubt that she would have felt the same way had she been in the other's shoes. "Cam did tell us about you that first day. True, at first, I think he did feel a little sorry for you and a little guilty. Not so much for you yourself but for the pain he had unwittingly inflicted on you with regard to your education and future plans. Later he came to respect the way you were single-handedly raising the twins. We all greatly admire you for what you have accomplished. He was afraid if you had known his name was Eastland, you would have refused his help." Kathleen ventured a sympathetic smile.

"The twins have truly been a joy to have around. Mother is going to miss them terribly, and it will almost be a sin to take them completely away from her. She has been so sad and withdrawn since Phillip died. Now she has something to look forward to every day." She paused, pleased that at least Chris was listening to what she was saying.

"Now that I've had my say on the subject, I will get to the real reason I came up here. You asked me what I needed that I couldn't get if I really wanted it. Well, it's true, maybe most things I really want, I can get. What I need from you no amount of money can buy. I need you and, of course, Jon and Jenny."

"Me? I don't understand." Chris was still angry, but she couldn't deny she was intrigued.

"I don't know if you know anything about the company Robert and I have. He is a civil engineer. He designs and builds bridges. We started it up two years ago. It has been a real struggle for us, but now he has a chance to go to England and build a set of bridges. It could mean the difference between us becoming a successful company and one just getting by," Kathleen explained.

"But that has nothing to do with me," Chris interrupted her, impatient to finish her packing and be gone before Cam returned home.

"Well, I am an engineer also, and I do most of the paperwork for the jobs. Robert says he needs me there, with him. If I don't go, he will turn the job down. I can't go unless I know my children are happy and well taken care of. I don't want to take them out of school since they are just getting settled. I need someone I know we can trust to live in our house and look after the children until school is out. We will be gone for several months, so they can spend some time with us during the summer. I don't think we will be back in time for school to start, so I'll need someone to get them started to school next fall. I worry about my children every time they are out of my sight but if you, Jon, and Jenny were to move into my house to care for them, I think I could handle being away from them for a little while. Chris, you have done such a wonderful job with Jon and Jenny that I have no doubt that you could handle anything that comes up, and I know that the children's welfare will always come first." Kathleen held her breath and waited for Chris to react to her plea.

"I don't know—I can't think right now." Chris knew she should turn the request down and make a clean break with the whole family, but there was something in Kathleen's voice that made her hesitate. The money she made doing that would help her to pay her debt to Cam sooner. Surely she would get paid!

"Please. At least consider it. I know you are angry at us, but anything Cam did was not intended to hurt you in any way. My request has nothing to do with anything that has happened. It's just me trying to look out for my children. The children get along so well that maybe it will help them not miss their father and me so much if they had Jon and Jenny to keep them company."

"Can't your mother look after them?"

"Mother loves the children dearly, but I can't ask her to take total care of them for several months. Jon and Jenny have been wonderful for Mother this last two weeks. I have seen such a change in her since they have been here. It has been really nice to hear her laugh with the children instead of sitting quietly in her room or by her roses. She knows this is only temporary, but I suspect it will be enough to get her interest back into doing other things. At one time she was very active in volunteer work, and now I hope she will do it again instead of being content to just sit."

"Please say yes, Chris. I can't imagine leaving my children with anyone else. In fact, I'm not sure I could. It will only be for a short while," Kathleen pleaded with Chris.

"I don't know what to do. I should be out looking for a job so I can start repaying some of my debts." Chris wanted to accept the position, but common sense told her that a paying job was more important to her immediate future than doing Kathleen a favor.

"Oh, this is a job offer." Kathleen quoted a salary that was almost double what she made at the factory. "Of course, there will be extra money for household expenses, and you will have a car at your disposal. You do drive, don't you?"

"Yes, I have a license." Chris was stunned at the offer. She would certainly have no money worries while she was there.

"Please don't think I'm doing this out of pity. If anyone's going to feel sorry for anyone, it will be me for myself if you turn me down." Kathleen felt Chris was wavering.

"Let me think about it and discuss it with Jon and Jenny. Maybe we can talk more later." Chris relented, ever so slightly.

When Ramona returned with the children, Chris called them to her room to tell them about Kathleen's offer.

"You mean we will live in somebody else's house? What would we do with our house?" Jon raised the first question.

"It will only be for a short while, and we won't be very far from home, so we can go check on it often."

"What about Luci? Will she know where to find us?" Jenny asked.

"I'll call her and tell her where we are so she can find us. How would that be?"

"I guess that will be okay." Jenny was satisfied.

"It might be fun having someone to play with after school. What do you think, Jen?"

Jon thought it would be a good idea.

"I like Sarah, so it might be fun. I guess it will be all right if you want to, Chris," Jenny agreed with Jon.

"I'm not really sure if I want to do this, but I just wanted to see what you two thought."

Chris still had some thinking to do before she came to a decision about the position. There was the matter of Cam's lies to her. Right now, she didn't ever want to see or talk to him again, but her heart kept telling her that he wasn't going to be that easy to forget.

She hadn't decided just whom she should be angry with. Cam for sure, but shouldn't she be upset with all of them for agreeing to go along with the lies? She liked and respected them all, but how could she not be angry with them? Maybe if she listened to their side . . .

"We'll talk to Kathleen again later, and maybe we can decide then."

Chris left the children to go in search of Ramona to thank her and tell her good-bye. No matter how she felt about her, Ramona had been very good to the three of them, and for that she was grateful.

"I'm so sorry that you are leaving like this. Kathleen told me about your conversation with Scott. I regret you had to find the truth out in that manner. We were only trying to help, not out of pity, but because we saw another human being in trouble and did what we could to ease the situation. We tried to get Cam to tell you the truth of who he really was, and he was going to, but he waited too long." Ramona apologized for her part in the deception. "Why don't you spend the night here and go home in the morning? It's late, and you won't have anything to eat until you go to the store, will you? If you are worried about seeing Cam this evening, don't be. He left word with Ellen that he wouldn't be home until very late."

"I need to call Luci to tell her I am going home. I guess it can wait until tomorrow."

"If you want, call her from here this evening. You might have a better chance of catching her there now than in the daytime," Ramona suggested.

"I guess it wouldn't hurt to spend one more night here. You're right about the food. If you are sure you don't mind, I will call Luci this evening."

At first there was no answer at the number that Luci had given her. On the third try a man answered. Chris asked to speak to Luci, and after a long wait she came on the line.

"Luci? It's Chris."

"Sis, where have you been? I've been trying for three days to reach you. Things aren't working out here. Frank wants me to get my own place. I can't find a job, and I'm broke! I need you to send me enough money to come home." Luci was too busy complaining to ask how Chris was feeling.

"I don't have much money. How much will a bus ticket cost?" She thought she could spare some if it wasn't too much.

"A bus ticket! I can't ride that far on a bus again! I want to fly!" Luci was shocked that Chris would even suggest such a thing.

"I'm sorry, Luci, but I can't afford plane fare. Tomorrow you call the bus station and find out how much a ticket will cost. I'm going home in the morning, so call me there. I'll wire you the money plus something for food on the way home." Chris quickly hung up before she had to listen to more complaining.

"I'm sorry, my dear, but I couldn't help but overhear your conversation. If you need money for anything, I will be glad to help out," Ramona offered, knowing Chris would most certainly refuse, but she had to try. "If you wish, you may consider it a loan, and no one else need know."

"No, thank you, Ramona. It won't hurt my sister one little bit to ride home on the bus." She owed the family far too much as it was. "Please excuse me. I want to go see what the children are doing."

"Certainly." Ramona smiled to herself as Chris left the room. It was good to see her show some spunk toward that sister!

Chris made sure she was in her room long before Cam was due home. When someone tapped on her door, she didn't answer. After a second knock, she heard footsteps leaving. She really didn't want to have a confrontation with him right now. In fact, she never wanted to see him ever again.

Cam generally left for work about eight, so she decided to wait until she was sure he was gone, before going down stairs. Someone knocked on her door early, but she pretended to be asleep. She heard the door open and footsteps as someone approached the bed, but she didn't move. Her visitor left as silently as he came. She knew it was Cam because she had grown used to the scent of his cologne.

"I'm glad you decided to stay the night," Scott greeted her as she entered the dining room, where he and Ramona sat having coffee. He rose to assist her with her breakfast from the sideboard.

"I'm leaving as soon as I can get through breakfast and call a cab," she informed him. She couldn't decide if she should be angry at him for his part in the reason for her leaving or thankful to him for getting everything out in the open.

"Are you sure I can't talk you out of going today?" Scott smiled, hopefully at her.

"No, it's time for me to leave this house and get on with my life." She knew she couldn't delay leaving any longer.

"Will you at least allow me to take you home?" Scott conceded defeat temporarily.

"Cam asked me to have you wait until he gets home before you leave. He wants to talk to you." Ramona knew what the answer would be, but she had to deliver the message.

"I don't think I want to talk to him just yet. Truthfully, I don't know what I would have done without your help. I just wish everyone had been more honest with me." Chris had been trying to sort out her feelings. She was sure that she was angry at Cam. Perhaps he alone should bear the brunt of her wrath. Perhaps the others were only going along with his lie because he asked them to. Yet they should have told her.

"We really did want to tell you the truth, but Cam didn't think you would have allowed us to help if you had known who we were," Ramona attempted once again to explain their actions. "He promised to tell you the truth, but then you had to have surgery, and he just kept putting it off so as not to upset you any more than you already were. Then it was too late, and you found out the truth. I do apologize for my part in the whole thing. I hope you can find it in your heart to forgive me. I do so admire the way you have raised Jon and Jenny. They have brought life back into this house, and for that I shall be eternally grateful for the time I have been allowed to spend with them."

"Of course, I forgive you! You've been so wonderful to the twins and me that I can't possibly be angry with you." Chris hugged Ramona, relieved to know how the older lady felt about having the children as her houseguests for so long.

"Scott, if you're sure you don't mind, I will let you take me home as soon as I can gather everything up. Luci is supposed to call later this morning, so I want to be there when she does."

As soon as she finished breakfast, Chris called the children to leave. They bid a sad farewell to Ellen and to their new "grandma." Chris had tried to discourage them from calling her that, but nothing short of absolute forbiddance would have stopped them, so she said nothing.

Scott borrowed his mother's car so there would be room for all their belongings. He drove it much like his sports car. Even Jon noticed he was going much too fast around corners. He didn't say a word, but when Chris looked back at them she noticed he was hanging on tight to Jenny's hand, and she had her eyes closed. Scott wasn't taking the chances, as he had in his sports car the day before, just driving too fast, so Chris said nothing. Very soon he stopped in front of her house, and she breathed a sigh of relief. At least she was home again. She helped the kids get their things out of the car, bid a quick thank-you and good-bye to Scott.

"Can't I come in for a while?" Scott asked.

"Not today. The house had been closed up for a while, so I need to air it out. Then I will have to go to the store to get some groceries," she put him off.

Scott seemed a little upset by her refusal but promised to come back soon and left, throwing gravel behind the car as he sped off.

"He sure doesn't drive like Cam, does he?" Jon stopped to watch Scott leave.

"No, he certainly doesn't." Chris paused for a moment to watch Scott's car tear down the road.

Chapter Six

She sent the children to put their things away while she opened up the windows so fresh air could enter the house.

True to her word, Luci called shortly after their arrival home. She gave Chris the cost of bus fare, plus she checked on plane fare just in case she could change her sister's mind.

While the twins were out checking on things in the backyard, Chris quickly made out a grocery list.

"Come on, kids. We need to go to the grocery store, or else we won't have anything for supper."

"When can we go back to our new grandma's?" Jenny asked while they were walking to the grocery store.

"I don't know, honey. We'll have to just wait and see." She doubted they would be returning there, but she didn't quite know how to explain why not, so she evaded the question for the time being.

"I'm going to miss the pool. I'm a really good swimmer. Even better than Bobby," Jon bragged.

"I'm going to miss Sarah," Jenny admitted a little sadly.

"You will see her at school, won't you? Besides, if I take that job with Kathleen, you'll both be living in their house," Chris reminded the both them.

"Oh yeah. I guess that's right. I forgot," Jenny exclaimed. This thought brightened the both of them considerably. While at the store, Chris wired the money to Luci.

Chris had serious reservations about taking the position Kathleen had offered. She had no doubt she could handle the responsibilities, but there was Cam. She really didn't want to see him again, but neither did she have any doubts that he would keep a close eye on his niece and nephew no matter who took the job while their parents were gone.

The doorbell rang just as she was finishing the dishes that evening. She opened the door to a big bouquet of flowers. Behind them stood Cam.

"Oh, it's you." She wasn't prepared to talk to him just yet.

"May I come in for just a moment? Please." He was prepared to plead his case on his knees if it came to that.

"I suppose, but only for a minute." She stepped aside so he could enter.

"Please accept these as a small token of a peace offering." He extended the flowers to her, all the while hoping she wouldn't throw them back at him.

"I'm truly sorry that I wasn't honest with you from the beginning. I have no excuse for what I did, except I thought you were in need of help, and I didn't think you would have taken it had you known who I was. I realize the birthday party and the play were flimsy excuses, but I really wanted to keep you in my life until I could figure out a way to help you. Actually, I thought you would kick me out on my ear when you found out the truth."

He ventured a small grin at her stern face. "When you practically fainted in my arms, I decided it might be better if you didn't know the truth. So then, I had to swear everyone else to secrecy. In all fairness, they tried to talk me out of it, but I thought I knew best. What I didn't count on was Scott coming home and blowing my cover before I got up the nerve to fess up to what I had done. Can you ever forgive me?"

Before she could form an answer, the back door flew open, and the twins came rushing in. As soon as Cam saw them, he dropped to one knee, and they wasted no time rushing into his open arms.

"I knew you would come to see us," Jon welcomed him.

"I was a little afraid you would forget all about us," a relieved Jenny added.

Chris thoughtfully watched the scene before her. It was difficult to be angry with someone the children adored so, and especially since it was equally obvious that he returned their love. In all fairness, she guessed she could understand how it happened.

Her pride probably would have forced her to turn down his help had she known who he was. But then, what on earth would they have done while she was in the hospital?

"Well, am I forgiven?" Cam grinned over the heads of the children.

"If they like you, I guess you can't be all bad." Chris sighed, but she wasn't prepared to let him completely off the hook just yet.

"You have to promise never to lie to me again, and I'm still waiting for copies of all the doctor and hospital bills. I want all those, and then we will talk about forgiveness."

"I promise I will never tell you anything but the truth from now on, but can't we forget about the bills and let them be my penitence for past sins?" It bothered him that she was going to have to struggle to repay him when he could well afford it. He knew that her pride would force her to repay every penny if he couldn't talk her out of it.

"No, I won't forget that big of a debt. Give me the bills, and I will think about trying to forgive you." She knew she had lost the battle of forgiveness, but she wasn't willing to admit it to him just yet.

"Okay, if you will let me come back, I will bring what I have." Cam sensed he was making headway. He released the children and stood up, grimacing as he straightened back up.

"Oh!" All of a sudden it dawned on her. If Cam's name was Eastland and his father owned the factory, then he must have been in that plane crash that killed his father. She couldn't remember exactly what his injuries had been, but she did remember that they had been severe.

"Oh what?" Cam looked at her curiously.

"What—oh it's nothing. I just had a thought." She was reluctant to ask him about the accident that took his father's life because she remembered how long it took before she could talk about the crash that took her parents' life, without pain.

The doorbell interrupted them. Chris excused herself to answer it. To her surprise, Scott was standing there holding a single white rose.

"A rose for a rose." He bowed, raised her hand to his lips, kissed the back of it ever so gently, turned it over, and laid the flower on her palm. His motions were so smooth that she was sure he had done that many times before. She couldn't help but wonder if it had ever worked.

"What are you doing here, Scott?" Cam demanded as he moved to stand beside Chris.

"Just checking on our little patient. What are you doing here?" Scott shot back, still holding onto her hand.

"I needed to talk to her, if it's any of your business," Cam answered.

"From what I heard, you should have done your talking some time back." Scott smirked at Cam. "It's a little late to do it now. If you will excuse us, Chris and I have some getting acquainted to do."

"Please, could you both leave? I'm very tired and it's been a long day." She, wanting to avoid the approaching confrontation, disengaged her hand from Scott's grip and stepped away from the both of them.

"Yes, I'm sure you are. I'm sorry. I should have realized that sooner. Let's go Scott."

"You go ahead, Cam. I'll be along in a little while," Scott stalled.

"Now, Scott! You can get acquainted, as you put it, later." Cam's voice left little room for argument.

"It's not going to wear her out to just sit and talk." He turned to Chris. "Is it, honey?"

"If you don't mind, Scott, I am rather tired. Could we do this later?" She could feel her head starting to ache.

"You heard the lady. She is tired. Let's go. Now!" Cam held the door open, waiting for Scott.

"Okay, Chris, I'll go, but only because you asked me to, and only if I can come back another time." Scott didn't like being turned down, but he agreed because he thought Chris was worth pursuing.

"Good night, fair lady. I shall dream of you tonight." Scott bowed again, turned on his heel, and strode past Cam with a triumphant look on his face.

"Take good care of your sister, kids." Cam turned to the twins, who had been standing wide-eyed, listening to the conversation.

"Good-bye, Cam," Jenny found her tongue.

"Chris, I apologize for upsetting you this evening. Sleep well, and maybe we can finish our conversation some other time." With that, he quietly closed the door.

Some time later she heard the squealing of tires. Obviously, Scott had waited until he saw Cam leave before he departed.

By the time Chris got the twins to go to bed, she was ready for bed herself. It felt so good to be in her own bed in her own little house. Ramona's was big and beautiful, but this house felt more comfortable to her.

Chris had asked Kathleen for a little time to think about the job offer before she gave a definite answer. Kathleen said they had a week to give a decision to the English company, so she promised an answer before that time. The only reasons Chris could think of for refusing the position were Cam and Scott. The latter she didn't feel entirely comfortable around; and she couldn't define exactly how she felt about the former, but somehow she knew her life would become extremely complicated if he remained in it.

The pay was extremely generous, and she had nothing else to do right now. There probably wasn't another job for that kind of money in her future. Maybe, if she was careful, she could use the money from this job to finish her credits at night school after all. The chance to finish her schooling finally persuaded her to take Kathleen's offer. Cam and Scott be hanged!

Kathleen hugged Chris for joy when she heard her decision to accept the job offer.

"I can't tell you how much this means to the whole family. Bobby and Sarah will be able to stay here and finish the school year, and I can go with Robert to help secure our future. Not that I won't worry every minute we're gone, mind you, but I will know they are being looked after by someone who truly cares for them and will always have their best interest in mind." Kathleen had her private doubts of Chris accepting the job, but she was oh so glad to be wrong!

"We will need to leave before too long. Could you come over to the house the last of next week? I think it might help if you were there a few days to learn their routine."

"Of course. Luci will be home tomorrow, so she can stay here and I won't have to close the house up again. Would Thursday be soon enough?" Chris asked.

"That will be great! I'll pick you up right after lunch," Kathleen agreed.

"Hi! I'm home!"

At the sound of Luci's voice, the twins forgot about the lunch they had been clamoring for a few minutes earlier, and rushed to greet their other sister.

"Luci, I sure missed you! I can't wait to tell you what happened to Jon and me while you were gone!" Jenny hugged Luci, anxious to tell her all about where they had been.

"We have a new grandma," Jon added, not wanting to be left out.

"Okay, kids, you can tell me all about it later. Where's Chris?" Luci looked up to see her standing in the kitchen doorway.

"Hello, Luci," she said quietly. "It's nice to have you home."

"Hi, Sis," Luci flashed Chris a big grin. "God, I'm tired. That bus ride was a killer. I think I'll sleep for a week. What's this about a new grandmother?"

"It's a very long story. Come have lunch and we'll fill you in." Chris set another plate at the table for her sister.

Jon told her about Bobby and Cam and his cars, and then Jenny told her about the birthday party and Sarah. Chris explained who they were and how they came to meet. She couldn't seem to find the right time to bring up the subject of Kathleen's job offer and her decision to accept it.

"If you two are finished, why don't you go out and play for a while? I think Luci might like to rest while I do the dishes." Chris got up to clear the table.

"Say, Sis, would you do me a favor while I take a nap?" Luci asked as soon as they were alone.

"Of course, what is it you want me to do?"

"Could you unpack for me? I'll go into your room to rest so you won't disturb me. Oh—I didn't get a chance to do laundry before I left New York, so do you suppose you could throw a few things in the washing machine for me?" Luci rose from the table, stretched, yawned, and continued. "Gosh, am I beat. I think I'll take a bath before I lie down."

"Go ahead, Luci. I'll take care of your things." She sighed. Luci would never change.

"When you get up we'll talk about the job offer I have."

"Yeah, we can talk later, when I am rested." With that she disappeared, leaving her sister to do the work. She had been so busy complaining about her life that she didn't once ask Chris how she was feeling.

Chris was in the kitchen starting dinner when Luci, fresh from her nap, came looking for her.

"I hope you don't mind that I put on your robe. I guess all of mine are still dirty," she said by way of a greeting.

"Of course, I don't mind. I'm working on your laundry, but there still are a couple of loads to do. You really must have a bought a lot of clothes while you were in New York."

"Yeah, my friend wanted me to look nice when we went out, so he bought most of them for me." Luci dropped onto a chair while Chris worked around the kitchen.

"I'm glad you are here so we can talk before the kids come in to eat." She quickly explained the situation to Luci. "So you see, I'm glad you are here so you can look after the house while I'm at Kathleen's with the children," she finished.

"But what is going to happen to me? I don't know anything about taking care of a house! I can't even cook!" She wasn't taking the news very well at all.

"Now, Luci, I'm sure everything will work out. I won't be very far away. Besides, it's high time you learned how to take care of yourself," Chris tried to reason with her sister. "I will have the use of a car, so I can come by often to help you."

"Why can't you take care of the kids here? You don't really have to go over there, do you?" Luci whined, afraid she might have to take over some of the responsibilities that she had always done her best to avoid.

"I have to go over there because that's where Kathleen wants her children to be. It's their home, and their parents feel they won't be as lonely if they are in familiar surroundings. We don't have enough room here anyway," Chris explained.

"When do you have to go?"

"Thursday afternoon. I'll have plenty of time to stock up on things you will need before I leave."

Their conversation ended just then when the door opened to admit two hungry children.

"Is dinner ready yet?" They asked as soon as they saw Chris at the stove.

"Almost. Wash your hands while I finish up. Luci, would you set the table?" Chris asked as she put the finishing touches to the food.

"Where's the stuff?" Luci sighed. She guessed she had better start learning how to do some things around here in case she couldn't talk Chris out of this harebrained idea of this job she was so set on taking.

Cam called often to inquire about everyone. She found their conversations lasted longer each time they talked. This time, when she got off the phone, she was surprised to find they had been talking for nearly thirty minutes. Cam was an easy person to talk to. She found that out during the evening visits he paid her while she was at Ramona's. He seemed truly interested in her and her family, no matter what the subject. He always knew what questions to ask to keep the conversations flowing.

Scott had returned on Sunday afternoon. This time he came armed with another rose for Chris and candy bars for the twins. They, disappointed that it wasn't Cam, dutifully thanked Scott and left as soon as Chris excused them.

For some reason, Jon and Jenny didn't like to be around Scott. Chris hadn't pressed the issue because she thought they would warm up to him once they spent time around him like they had with Cam. In all fairness, she had to admit they accepted Cam the first time they saw him, so maybe they could sense a difference in the two men.

"I came over to take you for a ride," he said as soon as they were alone.

"I don't think your car is big enough for the four of us." Chris pointed out. She was not particularly anxious to ride with Scott again.

"Can't the kids stay home by themselves for a while, or can't you get a babysitter or something?" he demanded.

"They are far too young to stay home by themselves, and I don't know anyone who would be free to sit on such short notice."

Though he tried not to show it, Chris could tell Scott was very angry at her refusal. He rose from his chair and started pacing around the room. Watching him, she guessed he rarely failed to get his way about anything.

"What about your sister? Isn't she here?" He stopped in front of Chris's chair.

"She's out for the day." For once, she was glad Luci was not home.

"Well! I guess I'll be on my way if you won't go out with me."

"Not won't, Scott. Can't," Chris explained.

"Same difference. I'll see you around." With that he left, and she hadn't seen him since.

Chris spent Wednesday catching up on laundry and stocking the kitchen shelves for Luci. She tried to show her where things were, but every attempt was met with a barrage of complaints about how she would be off having fun in a mansion while Luci would be stuck there alone. Finally Chris gave up. She figured Luci would survive even if she hated every minute of it.

Kathleen called Wednesday evening to confirm the arrangements for picking up Chris and the twins.

"If you are still sure you want all of us, we'll be ready right after lunch." She couldn't help but worry that something would happen to prevent her from taking the job.

"Are you kidding? It's all the kids can talk about! Bobby even cleaned half of his room so Jon would have space for his stuff." Kathleen had been half afraid that Chris would back out, so she was as relieved as Chris.

"I guess your sister got there safely?"

"Yes, she's here. She's going to take care of things here while I'm over there."

"That's good. I'm looking forward to meeting her. I'll see you tomorrow then. Goodbye." With that Kathleen ended their conversation. She was very curious as to what kind of a girl this Luci was. From what little she knew about her, Kathleen thought she had Luci pretty well figured out. Time would tell if she was right.

Luci had given up on the idea of trying to talk Chris out of taking the position. Instead, she chose to mope around, feeling sorry for herself. Since the death of her parents, Chris had taken care of the house, the cooking, and all of her needs. Now everything was going to fall on her shoulders, and she didn't like it one bit! Too bad she couldn't go with Chris. Say! That wouldn't be a bad idea! Somehow, she had to get a look at this house where Chris was going. She had to figure out a plan to accomplish that. Anything would be better than staying here by herself! There had to be a way.

"You must be Kathleen." Luci made sure she was on hand to open the door to Kathleen's knock the next day. "Hi, I'm Luci, Chris's sister. It's a pleasure to meet you."

"Hello, Luci. I'm glad to meet you," Kathleen responded.

"Hi, Kathleen! We're almost ready. I see you've met Luci." Chris came into the room carrying another bag to add to the pile by the door. "Luci, would you mind seeing where Jon and Jenny are?"

"Of course. I'm always glad to be of help whenever I can. It was nice meeting you, Kathleen."

"It's nice to finally have met you, Luci. Take care of yourself while Chris is at my house." Kathleen turned to open the door so they could start getting the luggage loaded into the car. That girl really knows how to turn on the charm, she thought to herself. Maybe she should try to be an actress instead of a model.

There was absolutely no doubt in Kathleen's mind that Luci hated the idea of being left there to fend for herself, and she would do anything she had to in order to find an excuse to move in with Chris and the children as soon as possible. Personally she had no objection to Luci doing that if that was what Chris wanted. It was going to be interesting to see just how she accomplished the move.

Chapter Seven

Chris and the children adapted to each other very easily and had soon settled into a routine. Luci called every day on one pretext or another and managed to wrangle an invitation to Sunday dinner.

As soon as Luci saw the house, she knew she had to move in. There would be plenty of room for her. The huge master bedroom would be vacant once Robert and Kathleen left. It would suit her needs very nicely.

"Have you ever had any problems with prowlers, Chris?" She started putting her plan in action at the dinner table while everyone was still seated.

"No, I've never heard anything, and I don't remember any of the neighbors having ever mentioned any problems like that," Chris answered.

"I heard a funny noise the other evening. It scared me so badly I didn't get a wink of sleep all night. I haven't slept very much since then. I keep hearing strange noises outside my bedroom window." Luci turned to Robert and continued. "I'm a real coward when it comes to staying by myself. I guess I had better get used to being there all alone, with nobody to help me," she finished, sighing dramatically.

There it was! Kathleen had been waiting to see what sort of plan Luci would come up with. She had to give the girl credit; as devious plans go, this was a pretty good one.

Fortunately for Luci, Robert took the bait, and before anyone could say a word, he had invited Luci to stay with Chris while they were gone.

"I'm so sorry, Kathleen. I didn't mean for this to happen. I hope the fact that Luci will be here won't change your plans," Chris apologized for Luci's behavior. "I promise I will always give the children my full attention."

"No need to apologize for your sister's actions. To tell the truth, I'm not really surprised that Luci wants to move in here. You haven't talked about her very much, but when I met her, she didn't strike me as a person who was fond of living alone. Of course, her living here doesn't change anything. I have complete faith in you and the fact that she is living here makes no difference, as long as you don't mind."

Robert and Kathleen bid a tearful farewell to their children the end of the following week. Luci moved into their bedroom the next day, thanks to Scott's efforts.

"He's the best looking man I've ever seen, Chris. Do you like him?" Luci stood at the window watching Scott's car leave.

"Not especially," Chris dismissed her question without a thought.

"He's mine then. He has to have money to drive a car like that. I wonder what he does for living. Do you know, Sis?" Luci asked.

"I don't know exactly. I think he has something to do with the Eastland factory," she answered absently.

"I guess I'll make it my business to find out. He's too cute to pass up." Luci sat, drumming her fingernails on the window sill, plotting her next move.

Cam stopped by the next evening to see if everything was going all right.

"Cam, this is my sister, Luci," Chris introduced them.

"Hello, Cam. Any friend of Chris's is bound to be a friend of mine. I'm so glad to meet you." She held onto Cam's hand as long as he would allow before he withdrew it.

"Hello, Luci. It's very nice to meet you."

"If everything is in order here, Chris, I'll be on my way. Good night ladies." After a long look at Chris, he took his leave.

"I can't believe it, Sis! You are surrounded by good looking men. What does this one do?" Luci questioned her sister.

"He is half owner in some company, but right now I think he is managing the Eastland factory."

"Are you interested in him?" Luci asked.

"No! Absolutely not!" Chris quickly denied any interest.

"I can't believe my luck! Two rich men to choose from!" Luci smiled to herself, her thoughts awhirl. "Which one do I want? Did you say Cam owns his own company?"

"I think he told me he owned half of it. He has a partner."

"What kind of company?"

"I don't remember. It had something to do with computers, I think." She couldn't remember exactly what Cam had told her.

"A computer company. Hmmm. What did you say Scott did?"

"I'm not sure. Something to do with the Eastland factory. Why? Is that important?"

"Scott looks like he has money, but I bet Cam has more with his own business and all. I'll tell you what. Why don't we share them? I'll take Cam and you can have Scott. That way, we will both have it made!"

Luci wasted no time putting her plan into effect when Scott arrived the next morning.

"Hi, Scott. You're just the person I wanted to see," she greeted him as soon as she opened the door to his knock.

"Good morning, Luci. What do you need?" Scott looked around in hopes of seeing Chris.

"It's Chris. I think she needs some time out of the house and away from the kids. I was hoping you could take her for a ride. She's been looking kind of tired lately, and I'm sure a little fresh air will do her a world of good."

"Who's looking tired, Luci?" Chris entered the room in time to hear the end of the conversation.

"You are. I was telling Scott that I thought some time away from this house might help you to feel better." Luci turned to face Chris and winked.

"I'd be happy to give you a change of scenery, Chris. Grab what you need and we're off. I have the top down, and the open road is waiting." Scott had been trying to get Chris alone since that day on the bluff, and this was his chance!

"Scott, I'm sorry, but I can't leave the children alone when I promised their parents that I would take good care of them." She searched frantically for an excuse not to go. She didn't want to hurt his feelings, but she really didn't want to go with him.

"Oh go on, Chris," Luci jumped in. "I can certainly watch the children for a few hours. I need to start doing something around here to earn my keep."

"See? Your problem is solved. There's no reason for you not to get away for a while."

"We'll stop for lunch while we are out." Scott curled his arm around her shoulders in an effort to propel her toward the door.

"Go, Chris. I won't take no for an answer." Luci practically pushed the two of them out the door.

"I have to be back by three." Chris couldn't fight the both of them. Maybe it wouldn't be so bad. "Scott, you have to promise me that you won't drive too fast."

"I promise to have you back on time, and I promise to drive slow enough to please your grandmother if she were with us." He solemnly crossed his heart. The action brought a smile to Chris's lips, as it was designed to do.

"Well, that was easy," Luci said to herself as she watched the little red sports car take off with tires spinning.

"Now I have to work on Cam. That shouldn't be too difficult."

"Scott, you're driving twenty miles an hour over the speed limit. You promised to be careful." It hadn't taken him long to break his promise. For the second time, she was regretting her decision to go out with Scott.

"Don't worry. I always drive like this. I know what I am doing," Scott assured her, laying his hand on her knee.

"What about police radar? Aren't you afraid you'll get stopped?"

"It wouldn't be the first time." He chuckled. "But they have to catch me first. This little jewel will do a hundred and twenty-five. Usually I can give them the slip. Would you like to see just how fast she will go?" He reached over to again squeeze her leg. This time, taking his eyes off the road long enough for the car to drift over the center line.

"Please slow down! I don't care how fast you can go. I just want to get back home in one piece, preferably at or below the speed limit!"

"Don't be such a wet blanket, doll. I know how to drive. Haven't had more than four or five wrecks in my whole life," Scott scoffed at her fears.

He finally did slow down a little, but only after several pointed reminders and an outright threat by Chris to get out of the car and find her own way home.

They finally got home a little after five, to four hungry children and a very angry Luci.

"Where have you been? Cam called a little while ago to say he was stopping by after while. I told him you were outside so he wouldn't know you were gone. The kids are starving, and I haven't had a chance to get ready for him."

"I'm sorry, but I couldn't get Scott to bring me home any sooner. Go get dressed, and I will take care of dinner." Chris apologized and headed for the kitchen with the hungry children right on her heels.

She was cleaning up the kitchen after dinner when Cam arrived. He came in through the back door and perched on one of the bar stools to talk while she finished her work.

"Are you getting along okay?" he asked after a moment.

"Yes, I think so. The children seem to be adjusting well. They go back to school in the morning, so that will keep them busy most of the time. That should help."

"If you ever need anything, all you have to do is call me. I hope you know that," he reminded her and hoped she would listen to him.

"Yes, I know and I appreciate the offer." For the most part, she had forgiven Cam for his deception. His explanations had finally gotten through to her. She hated to admit it, but his reasoning made sense. She probably would have reacted just as he said, and then where would they have been? This way, temporarily at least, she didn't have to worry about a thing except keeping four children happy.

"Why, Cam. I didn't hear you come in. I've been playing with the children in the den. They do get on nicely together," Luci interrupted their conversation as she came bursting into the room, brushing against Cam as she took a seat next to him.

"You don't need me to do anything right now, do you, Sis?" Luci turned innocent eyes on her sister.

"Not that I can think of." The question surprised her because, except for this afternoon, Luci had not offered to lift a finger to help with anything.

"Cam, do you suppose that I could impose on you to take me to my house to pick up some things? I could go tomorrow, but I really need some of them tonight. I had intended to go this afternoon, but Chris was out with Scott, and I just couldn't leave the children."

"So that's where he disappeared to this afternoon." Cam wanted to ask where they had gone but decided it would be better to hold his tongue, for now.

"He stopped by here, and we thought Chris needed some fresh air, so he took her out for a little while," Luci added.

"Have you been feeling poorly, Chris?" He turned a critical eye on her.

"No, I've been feeling just fine." She didn't know quite how to explain her afternoon trip, but right now she could cheerfully have strangled her sister!

"Of course, I'll take you anywhere you want to go." Cam turned back to Luci. Two could play this little game. If Chris wanted to run all over the country with Scott, then he certainly could take Luci for a ride. "If you're not in too big of a hurry to get back, we can take a drive through the city park. I haven't been there for a long time."

"That would be great. I haven't been there in simply ages. And I am in no hurry at all to get back home." Luci breathed a sigh of relief because her plan was working better than she had hoped! She gave Chris a big wink over her shoulder as she and Cam left.

Luci continued her plan as the days passed, although she found more resistance than she expected from everyone except Scott.

Every time Luci pushed Chris toward Scott, Chris found excuses not to go, and every time Luci asked Cam to take her somewhere, either he didn't have the time or he took some of the children with them.

Ramona invited everyone over for a brunch one weekend. Cam caught Chris alone on one of those rare occasions that Luci wasn't lurking around close. He told her about a new play at the theater they had attended before she went to the hospital.

"I have two tickets, and I was wondering if—well I know how much you enjoyed the other play, so I thought maybe—if you want to, that is, we could go next Saturday night. Ramona has offered to keep the kids overnight." He was as nervous as a schoolboy but couldn't for the life of him figure out why.

"I don't know. I did enjoy the other play. Yes. If Ramona doesn't mind, I would love to see the play with you," Chris happily accepted the invitation.

"Play? What play?" Luci had been searching for Cam when she finally found them sitting in the den.

"Cam has tickets to a new play in town and asked me to go see it with him."

She would rather Luci hadn't found out about it quite so soon, but the damage was done.

"Who's going to keep the kids?" she demanded. She certainly wasn't going to watch the little brats while Chris was out with her boyfriend!

"Ramona's going to keep all of them overnight," Cam explained, feeling the same as Chris about Luci's knowledge of their plans.

"Good. When are you going?" A question neither Cam nor Chris wanted to answer.

"Next Saturday night." Chris finally responded.

"I guess you're probably going out to eat first?" she asked.

"I don't know. Why?" Chris recognized the gleam in her sister's eyes. Luci was up to something! The question remaining was, what was she up to?

"I was just curious. That's all." With that Luci left in search of Scott.

Luci and Scott were deep in conversation when Cam and Chris rejoined the group by the pool. The children were making full use of the pool while they were there.

"The brunch was delicious, Ramona. Please give my compliments to Ellen. Thank you again for inviting us," Chris again expressed her appreciation for the morning.

"You're welcome, my dear. It's nice to have the children back again. I've missed them." Ramona leaned back contentedly in her chair, watching the children at play.

"Did I tell you I have returned to doing some volunteer work?" Ramona changed the subject.

"No. I'm glad for you. What sort of things do you do?" Chris asked.

"Right now, I go to the convalescence home near the hospital three days a week. I write letters, run errands, sometimes just sit and talk or do whatever else I can do to make myself useful. It certainly feels good to be active again," Ramona explained, "I didn't realize how much I missed doing things like that for people."

Chris noticed Scott leave shortly after they arrived, and now he returned, stopped to say something to Luci, and they both came over to where the rest of the group sat.

"Guess what! Scott was able to get tickets to that play for next Saturday. Isn't that great?" Luci couldn't wait to tell Chris.

"I just called the theater. They said you hadn't picked up your tickets yet, Cam, so I asked them to cancel your reservations and give us four seats together. We are farther back and off to one side, but at least we can all sit together," Scott, proud of his ingenuity, explained just how he had accomplished it.

"Best of all, Scott called and found out where Cam had made reservations for dinner and cancelled the reservations for two and asked for a table for four." Luci intended to spend the evening with Cam even if Scott and Chris had to be there too!

That wasn't the evening he had planned! Cam didn't know if he was more upset with Scott or Luci! There was nothing to be done now but go along with their plans. Next time he would do a better job of keeping his plans to himself. If there was a next time!

※

Luci spent most of the next week searching for the perfect dress. She borrowed money from Chris to pay for it, the matching shoes, and evening bag.

When Kathleen made her weekly telephone call, Chris explained their plans for the play and hesitantly asked if she could borrow the dress she had worn to the theater before.

"Honey, you can't wear the same dress! Go to Mother's and pick out one of the others you tried on before. Anyone of them will be perfect. Go and have fun!"

Reluctantly, Chris agreed to choose another gown. She had to admit she felt a certain amount of euphoria when she tried on the gown she chose. It, like the blue one she wore to the first play, was a beautiful dress.

Luci spent the whole day preparing for the evening. First the beauty parlor for a manicure and hair styling; then a long soak in a bubble bath, her hair carefully wrapped so the curls wouldn't droop; then a nap so she would feel fresh for the evening ahead of them.

By the time Chris got the dresses pressed, the children fed their lunch and delivered to Ramona's, she barely had time to take a quick shower and get dressed. The rest of the time was spent helping Luci into her finery.

Promptly at five thirty, Cam and Scott arrived.

Luci had been pacing the floor for half and hour, afraid to sit down, lest she wrinkle something before Cam saw it.

"Can you get the door, Luci? I'm not quite ready." Chris called to her sister as she hurriedly transferred some things into the evening bag she had used before.

"Hurry, Chris, we don't want to be late," Luci said as she opened the door.

"My, don't we all look nice." Luci did a pirouette so the men could see her from all angles.

"Fantastic!" Scott, at least appreciated her new dress.

"You both look very nice," Cam finally commented as Chris entered the room. He couldn't take his eyes off Chris. She was even lovelier in her turquoise dress than that first night when she wore that blue gown.

"Sorry, I'm late. I just had a few last-minute things to do. I guess we had better get going." She was embarrassed to have Cam staring at her.

As soon as Luci saw Cam open the front door of the car for Chris, she knew she had to do something.

"Chris, would you mind if I sat in front? You know I get carsick sometimes when I'm riding in the back seat."

"When did that start bothering you, Luci?" She had never mentioned it before, at least not to Chris.

"I've been troubled with it for years, but lately it's been getting worse," she explained as she slid into the front seat, effectively forcing Chris into the back seat beside Scott.

"Get in, Chris. I promise to keep you amused." Scott grinned as he patted the seat beside where he was sitting. Chris reluctantly allowed Cam to assist her into the rear seat. She sat as far away from Scott as she could, but it didn't do her any good because he immediately slid across the seat to pin her against the door.

The table where they were seated at the restaurant was a far cry from the intimate one she and Cam had shared that earlier night. It was in the center of the room, surrounded by other tables. Cam assisted Chris into her chair, leaving Luci to Scott.

As Chris gazed around, she realized her memory had not done it justice. The colors were softer, and the foliage more lush.

"Good evening, sir. It's a pleasure to have us again. We hope you enjoy your meal," the waiter greeted them as he passed a menu to each.

"Hello, James. I always look forward to dining here, I'm sure it will be excellent, as usual," Cam returned the compliment.

"Would you like drinks, before dinner?" James asked.

"Bring me a martini. Heavy on the gin," Scott wasted no time placing his order.

"I believe I will have sangria," Luci decided.

"Would you like something, Chris? A glass of wine, perhaps?" Cam asked.

"I don't know. I've never tasted wine," she finally admitted, a little embarrassed.

"If you want, we could order you something very mild. If you don't like it, you certainly don't have to drink it," Cam suggested.

"If you will pick something out for me, I would like to try wine," a relieved Chris allowed Cam to choose her drink.

"Please bring us both one of your finest light wines, James."

"Very good, sir. I'll pick out a very special one for you." James bowed slightly as he took his leave.

At first taste she thought the wine was awful, but she was reluctant to admit it, so she decided to drink all of it whether she liked it or not.

"Actually, this is not too bad," she had to say something after she noticed that Cam was watching her.

"This is an excellent vintage." He smiled at her. "I noticed you are swallowing a little easier with every sip. Wine generally takes a little getting used to, but usually its taste will grow on you. If you truly don't like the way it tastes, please don't force yourself to drink it on my account. There's certainly no disgrace in not liking wine," Cam gave her a chance to leave her drink.

"I don't know if I like it yet or not, but I don't dislike it all that much. I want to finish this glass before I decide," Chris replied, happy to have been given a choice.

Luci and Scott were on their second drink before Chris finished her first.

Cam checked his watch and then signaled for James to take their order.

"I'm going to have the lobster." Again Scott was the first to order.

"That sounds deliciously expensive! I think that's what I will have." Luci followed his lead.

Cam waited for Chris to decide.

"Could I have the same thing I had last time? I can't remember what it was called."

"Of course, it that's what you want. But if you prefer you could also have the lobster or something else on the menu," Cam suggested.

"No, I don't want lobster!" Of that she was sure.

"Oh come on, Chris, try it. It's too expensive not to be good," Luci insisted.

"No lobster for me. I read somewhere how they cook them, and I think that's cruel. I could never deliberately cause a death like that."

"Come on, Chris, everything has to die before you eat it." This from Scott.

"If you want the chicken, that's what you should have," Cam interrupted the conversation.

"Please that's what I would like." She was glad to let Cam order for her again. And as he did the first time, he ordered the same for himself.

Chris was surprised to see that Luci was very adept at eating lobster. She didn't know her sister had ever eaten it before.

As before, the dinner was superb. And as before she couldn't decide on a single dessert, so she settled on a small piece of frozen lemon dessert, and because Cam had chosen it before, she asked for a small piece of chocolate cheesecake.

Cam once again had the chocolate cheesecake. Scott chose a baked Alaska, and Luci picked a strawberry tart, piled high with ice cream.

Again, Cam checked his watch and signaled James, who immediately brought their check.

"It's all yours, Brother dear," Scott informed Cam before he could suggest otherwise.

After giving his brother a sharp look, he signed the bill and rose to his feet.

"It's time to go," he said, as he moved to stand behind the chair in which Chris was seated, leaving Luci to Scott again.

The theater seats were far from the stage, so the view wasn't nearly as good as the first time, but that didn't matter to Chris. With the aid of a pair of opera glasses Cam had brought with him, she could see very well.

Once again, Cam outmaneuvered Scott and seated Chris next to himself. That way if she had any questions, he would be able to answer them.

The play had Chris's full attention from the beginning to the end. This story, unlike the earlier one, was a light comedy. For a short span she was transported into the land of make-believe.

Luci lost interest in the play after a few minutes, as did Scott. The two of them spent the better part of the evening looking around at the other people attending the play and whispering to each other.

When all was said and done, Chris considered the evening a success. Their dinner had been exceptional and the play, delightful. She felt a little more comfortable around Cam each time she saw him, and even the presence of Scott and Luci didn't take the edge off her enjoyment of the evening.

"How could you do that to me?" Demanded an angry Luci as soon as Cam and Scott left after dropping the girls off at home.

"Do what? I don't know what you're talking about." Chris thought it had been a good evening for everyone.

"Why did you take over Cam and stick me with Scott? You know I want Cam. Scott is the one you should have been paying attention to!"

"I didn't take over Cam. If you recall, at the restaurant, the table was square so no one took over anyone, and at the theater, I sat down first, and I had no control over who sat next me. Besides, you rode in the front seat beside Cam every time we got in the car."

Chris calmly pointed a few things out to the upset Luci.

"Well, maybe you didn't exactly do anything on purpose, but it sure seemed to work out that way," Luci finally admitted. "The question now is, how do I get Cam more interested in me? There's got to be a way."

She was going to have to come up with a better plan. She already had some ideas.

"The first thing is for you to spend more time with Scott. He already likes you, so that won't be hard to arrange. But it will take some doing to convince Cam that he wants me."

Chris loved caring for the children. Bobby and Sarah missed their parents terribly at first, but their weekly conversations with them and the presence of Jon and Jenny helped them to adjust, so they were a relatively happy group. On the whole they were very little trouble.

Scott continued his frequent visits. Chris avoided being alone with him as much as she could, but with Luci there to help Scott's cause, she often got trapped into spending time with him. He was relentless with his attentions, but she did everything she could, short of being rude, to discourage his advances.

Luci was so obvious in her pursuit of Cam that he took to phoning Chris when he wanted to talk to her, stopping by only occasionally for a quick visit with the children.

⁂

By mid June, Kathleen and Robert missed the children so much they asked Cam to make arrangements for Chris to bring them for a visit.

"But, Cam! I don't know anything about traveling! I've never even been on a plane!"

Chris was panicked at the thought of traveling with two children by herself.

"Besides, who would take care of Jon and Jenny?" She didn't trust Luci to look after them.

"There's nothing to it," Cam tried to ease her fears. "I can get you on a direct flight. I'll put you on the plane, and Robert will be standing at the gate to meet you when you get off. As for the twins, they are invited to go with you. Now could anything be easier than that?"

"I don't have a passport," Chris stalled for time to think.

"I'll take care of that," Cam countered.

"How long do they want us to stay?" she asked. Maybe she could do this.

"Kathleen didn't say. I would imagine, at least a couple of weeks." Cam could feel her weakening, so he pressed his advantage. "When you come home, Robert will put you on the plane, and I will promise to be at the gate to meet you." Cam knew he had won.

She knew that Cam knew he had won, so she gave up the argument.

"I know how much the children miss their parents, so if you will make the arrangements and not make me change planes, I guess I can try to do it."

"That's my girl! I know you can do this." Cam didn't doubt that she was terrified at the prospect of traveling that far by herself, let alone with small children, but neither did he doubt her courage to do so for the sake of the children.

"What do you mean you may be flying to England?" Scott demanded. "When? What brought that about?"

"Robert and Kathleen want to see their children. Cam is checking into making the arrangements now." She had put off telling him about the trip, but he happened to overhear his mother talking about it.

"Why didn't you come to me for help?" Scott was pacing around the room, clearly angry. "I could have made just as good of arrangements as he will. Probably better because I would have sent you first class!"

"Because Robert had already asked Cam to make the arrangements before I knew anything about it," she tried to calm Scott. "I didn't have any say in the matter."

"Well, you don't have to go if you don't want to. If they think they have to see their kids, then let them fly back home!" Scott countered. "There's no sense in uprooting your life!"

"Uprooting whose life?" Luci entered the room in time to hear the last of Scott's tirade.

"She's going to England!" Scott stormed, sensing he would have an ally in Luci. "Can you believe it? She wants to drop everything to fly off and leave us here alone?"

"England? What in the world are you talking about?" Luci demanded. She didn't like the sound of this at all.

"It's not for absolute certain. I may be taking the children to see their parents for a short while." She had intended to break the news to Luci when they were alone. She didn't need Scott there to interfere with her explanation of the trip.

"Cam talked to me earlier, to see if I would go. He's checking now to see if he can make the arrangements. I guess he will call me later."

"I'm not staying here alone with Jon and Jenny while you are off somewhere having a good time!" Luci had already started complaining.

"You don't have to stay here! I have a great idea!" Scott broke in. "Why don't we all go to England together?"

"That would be just great!" Luci jumped at the idea.

"It's out of the question!" Chris wanted to choke Scott. "You know we can't afford for you to go. Where would we get the money for your plane fare, let alone the other things you would need?"

"Don't worry about the expense." Scott knew he could get the money from his mother.

"The whole trip is on me." He intended to be on that plane with Chris, no matter what the cost was or who had to pay for it.

"We can't just decide that all of us should go! I don't know if they have room for everyone," Chris stalled for time to think. She wished Cam were there. He would know what to say.

"They have plenty of room. I'll give Kathleen a call and tell her to expect all of us. There! It's settled." Scott and Luci exchanged triumphant glances.

"I'll call Cam and find out which plane you will be on so we can all travel together. That way we will be there to keep you company so you won't get lonesome."

"Why don't we wait a day or two? Maybe they will change their minds, and I won't even have to go." This was getting out of hand. Cam certainly wasn't going to be happy with this turn of events. She wanted a chance to talk to him first and try to explain.

"She's right, Scott. Let's not get too excited just yet. This whole thing might blow over." For once, Luci agreed with Chris.

When Cam stopped to see the children the next evening, Chris tried to explain the situation and apologize for her sister's part in it.

"I should have known he would pull something like this," Cam said after a moment.

"Do you want Scott to go with you?" Cam had to ask the question.

"There's no denying that I would feel better if someone were with me, but we can't afford a trip like that for Luci, and I'd feel funny about letting Scott pay for it. I am looking at my fare as part of my job, so it's all right, but it's different with Luci."

"Besides, where would we all stay? We can't all just swoop in on Kathleen. It would cost a fortune if some of us had to stay in a motel all the time we are there."

Not exactly the definite answer he was looking for, but he had to accept it for now.

"Let me talk to Robert. I have an idea that might work." With that, he went to visit the children before leaving.

"It's all set." Cam called her the next afternoon. "I talked to Kathleen, and she assured me there was plenty of room for everyone, and don't worry about Luci's fare."

"Are you sure she doesn't mind us all arriving at once? By the way, I will pay you back for the extra expense." Chris still wasn't completely convinced they all should go.

"I'm sure. In fact, she's calling her mother today to invite her too."

"Good. I hope she will go. It's too bad you can't get away," she blurted out before she realized how it sounded. "You know, so the whole family could be together," she hastily added.

"Will you miss me if I'm not there?" he asked after a moment of silence.

"It would be a shame if you had to stay here and work while everyone else was off having a good time," she deliberately misinterpreted his question.

"That's not what I asked," he persisted.

"Yes, I'll miss you," she finally admitted quietly. It was the first time she had admitted, even to herself, that she had come to look forward to seeing him.

"In that case, nothing could keep me here while you are in England. Peter can hold the fort down for a little while." Cam's spirits soared with Chris's small confession.

"I'm really glad you are going," Chris answered, puzzled by her feelings.

"Well—we'll—ah—talk later." Cam replaced his receiver, leaving Chris trying to sort out her feelings holding a dead receiver.

Luci was ecstatic when she learned Cam was accompanying them. He had been more elusive than she had anticipated, but now she was sure the only reason he was going was because she would be on the plane with him. At any rate, if things worked out, she would have his attention for the whole flight. It didn't once occur to her that he might have other ideas.

Cam made arrangements for the plane tickets and secured all the passports.

Chris relied on Ramona, who had jumped at the chance to go, for advice as to what to pack. Since it was mostly casual, she felt the twins' wardrobe and hers were adequate, but vanity forced her to buy a new traveling outfit. She told herself she really needed a new one, but deep down she knew it was because she wanted to look nice for Cam.

Luci's wardrobe was already extensive, but she spent every dollar she could wheedle out of Chris for new things. She gave Chris her old luggage so she could buy a new, better set for herself.

Chapter Eight

Ten days later, they were winging their way to England. Scott was upset that they weren't traveling first class, but he quit complaining after Cam told him, in no uncertain terms, to be quiet and just appreciate the fact that he was going at all.

Ramona, having traveled extensively, understood the problems of traveling that far with active children, so she came prepared to take the children under her wing and entertain them. She had games, puzzles, and coloring books purchased for the trip.

The children were calling Ramona grandma all the time now. Chris couldn't define her feelings about that at first, but at some point in time, she wasn't sure just when, she realized that no matter how she felt about it, the two families were irrevocably entwined.

As she watched the children busy with their projects, it occurred to her that Ramona was a different person than the one she had met on the day of Sarah's birthday party. There was no doubt the children adored her, and her reserve had been replaced by her obvious pleasure at being in the company of the children.

Chris watched the five of them for a few minutes longer to satisfy herself that she wasn't needed. Then she curled up comfortably in her seat and opened the book she had brought for the trip.

Cam was already at work on some papers he had removed from his briefcase, and Scott, after seeing that Chris was occupied, asked Luci to join him in watching a movie.

Chris appreciated Ramona's suggestion that she carry raingear for herself and the children on board with her because England greeted them with rain and fog.

After a joyous reunion between children and parents, Robert led the group though the airport to the luggage area. Cam and Scott picked up their rental cars while the luggage was being collected. As soon as everyone was settled in their cars, Robert led the small procession out of the airport parking lot and onto the highway that would take them to their temporary home about a half hour's drive outside London.

Kathleen asked Chris to join them and the children in their van. Luci grabbed the chance to ride with Cam, and Ramona joined Scott in his car.

"I borrowed a book from the library to read up on England when I found out I was actually coming here," Chris told Kathleen. "But it didn't come close to preparing me for the beauty of the landscape here. I've never seen anything like it."

"It is beautiful here. Totally different from anything we have in Florida. The only thing that gets to me sometimes is the rain. I like clear sunshiny days, and there are precious few of those here," Kathleen hastened to add. "Personally, I will be glad to get back home to good old sunny Florida."

"There are some fabulous things to do and see here. I want you to see Hyde Park, ride the subway, or tube as they call it here, see the changing of the guard at Buckingham Palace. And you won't believe the cathedrals! I could go on and on, but it would take forever just to tell you about everything, let alone go to see it."

"I want to see all I can, but I think it's more important that you spend time with the children while we are here," Chris added, remembering the reason for their visit.

"I think we'll have plenty of time to do both." Kathleen pointed ahead. "Up there is home sweet home, for now at least."

As soon as Chris got a good look at the house, she understood why there was room for everyone. It was a huge sprawling two-story mansion larger than anything she had imagined it would ever be!

"We didn't have any idea when we leased the house that it was so large," Kathleen said, laughing at Chris's expression upon seeing it. "We sort of rattle around in it. Now, I'm glad it's so big. There's plenty of room for everyone."

"Come on in, everybody. I'll show you to your rooms first and let you get settled in before we have dinner." Kathleen led the way into the house as soon as everyone arrived. "We'll have a grand tour of the place later."

"Is this what they call an estate?" For once, Luci was impressed with her surroundings.

"I guess you could call this an estate, but we only have use of the house. The owners built a new house over the hill from here, and they take care of the land surrounding the house itself," Robert explained.

The house was obviously very old and extremely well cared for. A wide staircase divided the second floor into two wings. Chris, Luci, Ramona, and the children were given the larger of the two. Cam and Scott shared the other with Robert and Kathleen. Chris insisted Ramona take the bedroom with a private bath, the children shared a bath, and Luci grudgingly shared one with Chris.

The view from the window in her room held Chris mesmerized. It was more peaceful than anything she could ever have dreamed of. Off to the right lay a small lake surrounded by cattails, its mirror surface temporarily ruffled by the arrival of local waterfowl. Cattle dotted the dimpled hillside surrounding the lake. To the left, a line of trees bordered the pasture. Everywhere she looked, the foliage seemed as though it must have been painted. The shades of green were so vibrant they surely couldn't have grown naturally on their own.

Then suddenly, the sun melted the fine mist away; and miraculously a whole new version of the scene before her came forth, causing it to take on a whole new look, just as spectacular in it's own way, but totally different.

She was unable to move from her spot in front of the window, completely caught up in the ever-changing scene, until a knock on her bathroom door brought her back from her thoughts.

"I love my room. How do you like yours?" Jenny burst in through the open doorway from the hall as Chris answered Luci's knock on the bathroom door.

"It's beautiful. I'll come see yours in a little while," Chris answered Jenny.

"My room is great, Sis." Luci entered the room, looking around to see if this room was any better than hers. "I'm going to get Cam to drive me around tomorrow. Why don't you see if Scott will show you some of the countryside too?"

"We'll see. First I had better get unpacked." Chris turned to open one of the cases resting on her bed.

"What have you been doing? I've already finished with mine, and now I am ready to look around this castle." Luci frowned, impatient that Chris was so slow.

"I guess, I got caught up in the scenery out the window and lost track of time. It will only take me a minute or two to hang up what I have to. The rest I can get later."

"Well, hurry up." Luci sat down to wait.

"Have you seen the boys?" Chris asked Jenny.

"Sarah's mom came up to get Bobby and her. Jon went with them, but I decided to wait for you."

"We'll go find them as soon as I finish here." Chris picked up the last dress to hang in the roomy closet.

Kathleen had directed everyone to the drawing room while they waited for dinner.

The floor-to-ceiling windows provided another panoramic view of the countryside. Chris was drawn to stand in front of them, to drink in this new vista.

"I can't wait to see some more of the country around here. Why don't you show me some of it tomorrow, Cam?" Luci placed a proprietary hand on Cam's arm as he stood with Robert and Chris, soaking up the ambiance of the country before them.

"We both have the day off tomorrow, so Kathleen and I thought we could show you all some of the sights around here," Robert cut in, having recognized Luci's ploy for what it was. He thought he knew Cam well enough to know he was interested in Chris, not her sister. He figured Scott and Luci were more of a match.

"Dinner is served," the housekeeper announced from the doorway.

"Where are the children?" Chris asked. She knew they must be starved by now.

"The daughter of our housekeeper had agreed to help with the children. She is going to act as a nanny while they are here, Chris, so you can have sort of a vacation too."

"Oh, Kathleen," Chris was touched. "I didn't expect you to do that for us."

"Don't worry, we will still have plenty of time to spend with them," Kathleen continued.

"Celia will mainly see to their meals and bedtime activities. I know you have always looked after the twins, but please let me do this. All I want you to do is enjoy yourself while you are here. Okay?"

"Let's go eat! I'm starved! How about the rest of you?" Robert turned from his spot at the window and led the way to the dining room, where a feast awaited them.

Cam held the chair for Chris, but Luci slipped into it before she got there, leaving Scott to seat Chris across the table from Cam.

Their housekeeper, Mrs. Sloane, was a delightful lady transplanted from Ireland some twenty-five years earlier upon her marriage to her English husband. She described each authentic dish as it was served, in the most endearing accent Chris had ever heard.

Celia brought the children into the drawing room to say good night later in the evening.

"How are you doing, sweetie?" Chris asked Jenny when she came over to kiss her big sister good night.

"I'm having a good time. I miss you but Celia is fun."

"She talks funny, but she's nice," Jon whispered into Chris's ear while he was bidding her good night. "She's going to teach us some new games tomorrow. I miss you too, but she will do if you can't be with us."

"Just remember, I won't be very far away. So if you need me, I will be right there. Okay?"

"Now, scoot off to bed and I will see you in the morning. Good night and sleep well."

Chris got one last hug from both of them before they left.

Cam watched her eyes follow the children out of the room. There was no doubt as to who had raised the twins. Luci barely noticed them as they came in the room. Her good nights had been purely perfunctory.

Robert and Kathleen shared their children's good nights, and Chris had been the recipient of a hug from each of them also. Kathleen knew that she had certainly been fortunate when she found Chris to look after her children while she and Robert were away.

"Cam?" Robert asked for the second time. Then he noticed the direction Cam's eyes were going, so he waited patiently for him to come out of his thoughts.

"Yes, Robert. Did you say something?" Cam snapped back to reality.

"I thought we would leave about nine in the morning. I'll take the van so we all can ride together, if that's all right," Robert replied, trying not to smile at what he had just seen. He never thought he would ever see Cam as moon-eyed over someone as he was with Chris. He was going to do his best to run interference for Cam and try to point Luci towards Scott every chance he got.

"There's this really great place I want us all to have lunch. I expect we will be gone most of the day because there's a lot to see." Robert had their day all planned.

"That's fine with me." Cam was glad to let his brother-in-law take charge of their entertainment for the duration of their stay.

"Mr. Sloane told us about this little eating place, and we have been going there every chance we get. The food is great, and the atmosphere is something else," Robert added.

⁜

"This is going to be a glorious day!" Luci gushed from her seat next to Cam on the van the next morning. It had taken some finagling, but she got the seat she wanted, and she planned to thoroughly enjoy every minute of the day with him.

"We sure got off to a good start anyway." Scott was happy because he had Chris beside him in the seat right behind where Cam and Luci sat, so Cam wouldn't be able to watch their every move.

Ramona sat in the front seat with Robert, and Kathleen sat directly behind him so everyone could hear as she acted as guide.

Every rise in the ground brought new scenery. Occasionally, the road wound past large obviously very old estate houses, complete with their own stables and what appeared to be miles of wooden fencing.

"Don't they ever build small houses over here?" Every house Chris had seen was at least two stories, and some of them could have passed for castles.

"Of course, they have small houses in England!" Kathleen laughed because she had asked the same question. "Just not in this part of the country. This area is mostly what they call landed estates, which means most of the people around here own a great deal of property. If you look closely, you will see that there are small cottages tucked in among the trees behind the main buildings." She pointed out a barely visible house, almost hidden in a thicket at the rear of the manor they were just passing.

"Most often, the full time employees of the landowner will live there because it's handy for their jobs."

Kathleen enjoyed playing tour guide. She missed the children, but they elected to stay with Celia, and she guessed it was for the best. They probably wouldn't have enjoyed a long ride just to look at scenery.

The eating place Robert had chosen for the group to have lunch turned out to be an authentic English pub, complete with its own dart room. A couple of the regulars invited the guys to join them in a friendly game of darts while they waited for their food. Having engaged in the art of dart throwing many times before, all three confidently accepted the invitation, fully expecting to trounce their opponents soundly. They returned to their table very shortly, quite glum. They were the ones trounced in short order.

"They weren't too shabby," Robert was the first one to make a comment.

"Not for a couple of—what did they call themselves? Amateurs?" Cam grinned, beginning to see the humor of the situation.

"If you ask me, we were set up and made fools of." Scott wasn't so forgiving. He failed to see anything funny about the whole thing.

"Cheer up." Robert patted his brother-in-law on the back. "It was all in good fun, and it didn't cost us anything but a little of our pride."

"It's time to forget about the dart game, our food is coming," Ramona broke up the discussion in favor of the meal.

On the way back they stopped at a shopping area, where local artists displayed their wares. Chris searched for something to take to Jon and Jenny. Finally she settled on a small bean-filled frog for Jon. It reminded her of the one he played with in their backyard. She was sure Jenny would love the soft fuzzy little lamb she picked out for her. Kathleen picked up similar items for her children.

Chris had seen a small charcoal drawing at the first place they stopped. She knew it was far too expensive for her to buy, but for some inexplicable reason her thoughts kept going back to it. As they passed the shop on their way back to the van, she asked to be excused for a moment so she could take one more look at it. The sketch was of a shepherd watching over his flock while they slept. Suddenly, she knew why she was drawn to it, and she had to have it no matter what the cost! The drawing reminded her of Cam and how he had watched over her family while she was ill. When she found the proper time, she was going to give it to him as a small token of her appreciation for all he had done for her and Jon and Jenny.

Scott was quiet and withdrawn on the way back home. As soon as they arrived there, he asked to speak privately with his mother.

"Chris, if you want to read while you're here, please feel free to help yourself to any of the books in the library. There is a wide selection, so I'm sure you will find something to your liking." Kathleen remembered that Chris had expressed an interest in literature.

"Thank you, I believe I will go pick one out and take it to my room as I go. I do like to read a little while before I go to sleep." Chris left to pick out a book on her way upstairs.

"Cam, I have a favor to ask of you. Well, actually there are two of them." Ramona's voice interrupted Chris's search for a book. Someone had left the door ajar between the library and the drawing room. She didn't want to listen to their conversation, but if she moved they might hear her and think she was eavesdropping, so she stood unmoving.

"Of course, Ramona. You know I will always help you if I can," Cam answered.

"Scott asked me for some money a little while ago. I gave him what I thought I could spare. I would appreciate it if you would loan him enough to tide him over until we get back home. Then, could you possibly see your way clear to give him back his position at the factory?" Ramona explained what she wanted of Cam.

"He had his chance at the factory. Everything was fine until he took over!" Cam exploded. "He embezzled money, then took off and left me to try to salvage what was left of the business. I had to put up some of my own cash just to keep the doors open. There is no telling how many lives his actions ruined because I had to lay them off. How can you ask me to give him his job back?"

"I had no idea it was that bad," a stunned Ramona answered quietly after a moment.

"I really didn't want you to know, but you have to understand why I can't put Scott in a position of power there again." Cam was already regretting his outburst of temper.

"For your sake, I'll see to all of Scott's expenses while we are here, but I won't give him money to blow on anything that catches his fancy, and when we get back home, I will expect him to get a job to support himself."

"That's fair enough, Cam. I thank you for being honest with me. I have only heard Scott's side of things. It didn't once occur to me to ask for your side. For that, I am truly sorry. I will find Scott and explain things to him."

"That won't be necessary. I'll talk to him." Cam and Ramona must have left the room because she heard no further sounds. Although the conversation had been enlightening, she didn't wish to hear anything else; so grabbing the first book she came across, she quickly fled the library to the safety of her bedroom.

Everyone was gathered in the drawing room by the time she returned downstairs.

"Did you have a nice rest, my dear?" Ramona greeted her as she entered the room.

"It was fine, thank you," she replied as her eyes were drawn to Scott, who was pacing the floor like a caged animal.

"Where have you been?" he demanded as soon as he saw her. "I've got to get out of here for a while, and I want you to come with me."

"It's almost dinnertime," Ramona suggested. "Can't it wait until after we've eaten?"

"It might be better if you did wait a while before you go for a ride with him." Cam moved to her side and spoke softly so that only she could hear him. "I think he needs to cool off a little while before he gets behind the wheel."

"I'm going now! Are you coming with me or not?" Scott moved to stand directly in front of Chris, his hands on his hips.

"I'm sorry, Cam, but I'd better go with him. I know I can calm him down. He'll listen to me." Chris turned back to Cam before she left the room. "It'll be okay. We won't be gone too long."

<hr />

"Scott, you shouldn't drive this fast on a road you aren't familiar with! There are too many curves," Chris tried to reason with Scott in order to get him to slow down.

"I'm tired of being treated like a child! Just sit there and be quiet! Don't you try to tell me what to do like everyone else is doing! Just leave me alone!"

Chris closed her eyes as they slid around yet another curve. Suddenly she felt the car leave the ground. The last thing she remembered was flying through the air, and then there was darkness.

Chapter Nine

A low moan brought Cam to his feet and by her side. He wanted to be there for her when she woke up. He knew she would be frightened when she discovered she couldn't see.

They had all been there, off and on during the last five days, but Cam had steadfastly refused to leave her side.

According to the police report, the car had left the road at the top of a steep grade, sailed through the air for about twenty-five feet, landed on its wheels, at which point Scott had been thrown clear of the vehicle, before it rolled another one hundred fifty feet, and came to rest against a tree, impaled by one of it's lower branches. The seatbelt probably saved her life, but it may have also been the cause of some of her more serious injuries.

The branch had caused severe injuries to her face and eyes. The doctors operated on her eyes and sewed up her deepest cuts as best they could. Her doctor said they wouldn't know how successful they had been in saving her sight for several days. As for her other injuries, her broken arm would heal, but the doctors said it was too soon to know just how badly damaged the spinal column was. Only time would tell if she would ever be able to walk again.

Except for a few cuts and bruises, Scott had escaped injury. He had gone to see Chris the day after the accident but had not returned. He said he couldn't bear to face her after what had happened.

Ramona spent most days at the hospital, but at Cam's insistence she returned to the children at night. The children, especially Jenny, were taking Chris's absence very hard, and Ramona seemed to be the only who could console them.

When Chris had been hospitalized before, they had been allowed to see her every day and talk to her on the phone whenever they wanted to. Suddenly, there was no contact with her at all. They didn't understand why and were afraid to ask.

Cam returned to his chair when she made no further sound.

Some time later, she moaned again, this time turning her head. In an instant he picked up her good hand.

"Where am I? Why is it so dark in here? I can't see anything." Her voice was tinged with fear.

"It'll be all right, Chris. It's me. I'm here. I'll always be here for you." Cam squeezed her hand trying to give her the courage to face her future, whatever it might be.

"What happened? Where am I?"

"You were involved in a car accident, and now you are in the hospital."

"How are Jon and Jenny? Are they okay?"

"They are fine. Ramona and Luci are looking after them."

"Where are they?" She was trying to sort things out in her mind.

"They are at Robert and Kathleen's with Bobby and Sarah."

She was quiet for a few minutes, trying to remember exactly what happened.

Cam's firm grip helped to keep her panic at bay.

"Why can't I move?"

"Because you have bandages on your face and head and your arm is broken, so it's in a cast." He decided to tell her the truth when she asked because he had promised her he always would, and he knew she would accept nothing less.

"Can you turn on a light? It's so dark in here."

"It wouldn't help. You have bandages over your eyes," he finally answered.

"Why?"

"You had a discussion with a tree, and I'm afraid you lost." He tried to sound cheerful as he squeezed her hand, attempting to give her courage.

"Are you trying to tell me that I'm blind?" she asked quietly after a moment of silence.

"No, I'm not telling you that. The doctor says there is a good chance you will see again, but we won't know for a few more days."

"What else is wrong with me? I may as well know what I'm up against." She needed to know the worst.

"Why don't you let me call the doctor? He can explain it better than I can." He tried to put that conversation off for a while.

"I would rather hear it from you. Please?"

"Well, you have a lot of cuts and abrasions on your head and upper body. You will need some plastic surgery, but when that's done the doctor says you will look as good as new. Your broken arm will be fine in a few weeks when the cast comes off." He stopped, debating with himself as to how much he should tell her right now.

"There's more. Please tell me, Cam. I have a right to know."

"You have a damaged spinal cord. Only time will tell just how much, if any, permanent damage has been done." There! He had said it out loud!

"Are you trying to tell me that I'm paralyzed? That I will never walk again."

"We don't know that. The doctor said it would take time to determine what will happen."

"But it is a possibility?" Chris asked numbly.

"The only possibility I want you to accept right now, is that you will see again and that you will walk again! I don't want you to even think of anything less. Is that clear?" He had to do something to ward off the panic he could hear, creeping into her voice.

"When you put it that way, I can almost believe it." Chris managed a small smile through her bandages. "You did promise me you would only tell me the truth, and I am going to hold you to that promise."

"That's my girl. You and I are in this together. I want to be sure you know that whatever the future holds for you, I will be here to help in any way that I can." Cam hoped she believed that he meant what he said.

"Thanks. That means a lot." Chris had no doubt that he meant exactly what he said, and that fact was the only thing between her and utter desolation.

The next few days passed in a blur, for Chris. She remembered talking to Ramona, Luci, and Kathleen occasionally, but every time she woke and reached out, Cam was there to take her hand.

"How is Scott?" She remembered being in the car with him, so he must have been in the accident. No one had mentioned him, so she had to ask even though she was afraid of the answer.

"Except for a few minor cuts and bruises, he wasn't hurt," Cam answered.

"He was lucky." She was relieved for Scott.

"You might say that," Cam shot back tersely.

"Don't blame him too much. He was upset, and I should have tried harder to calm him."

She didn't want what happened to be the cause of a rift between the two men.

"How is our patient feeling today?" A nurse entering the room, pushing a cart, saved him from having to respond.

"I'm feeling better every day," Chris responded to the familiar voice.

"How would you feel about losing some of your bandages today?" she asked as she positioned the cart beside the bed.

"I'd love to lose all of them, but I'll settle for any that you can take off."

"The doctor will be here in a few minutes to take the ones off your eyes." She reached over and patted Chris's leg, forgetting for the moment that she couldn't feel her touch.

"If you want, Mr. Eastland, you may wait outside," the nurse suggested.

"No, Cam! Please stay with me!" She was afraid to face this alone, in case he took them off, and she still couldn't see.

"Now, Chris, I want you to keep your eyes tightly closed until I tell you to open them. We have darkened the room as much as possible, but you are still going to have to get used to the light gradually." Carefully, the doctor snipped the bandages off her eyes.

"Now, slowly open them. Not too fast though," he directed her as he lifted the last of the bandages from her eyes. "Now take your time, blink a few times before you try to keep them open. Things will be blurry at first, so don't expect too much right now," he cautioned her.

The first few times she cracked her eyes open, Chris saw nothing but a blur, then things began to get clearer. All at once, a curtain lifted, and she was able to see Cam's face at the foot of the bed, where he had stationed himself so he would be the first person she saw. A feeling she thought was gone forever suddenly came flooding back. Happiness. She could see! And the first person she wanted to see was right there! Right in front of her. Briefly she wondered if he stood there because he wanted that also.

"Cam! You look great!" She drank in the sight of him, and then added, with a small grin, "Well, to be perfectly honest, you look terrible. I think its time for you to go home and get a good night's sleep for a change."

"Oh, Chris" was all he could manage.

"Well, young lady. Everything looks fine. I don't think we have to worry about your eyes anymore." The doctor announced after completing his examination, the next morning.

"Now it's time to start some serious therapy on the rest of your body."

"What good will that do if I'm paralyzed?" Chris asked tonelessly. She had just received one miracle. She thought it was too much to ask for a second one.

"We don't know that you are paralyzed." The doctor gave her a sharp look and shook his finger at her. "Until we know for certain, one way or the other, I will not allow you to think negative thoughts. Your attitude counts for more than you can possibly imagine. Is that clear?"

"Do you really think there is a chance that I can walk again?" A tiny glimmer of hope shot through her body.

"What I am saying is that there is a vast difference between temporarily having no feeling and being paralyzed. Right now I am betting on the former, and I would feel a whole lot better if you were on my side. What do you say?"

"Doctor, I have a younger brother and sister who depend on me. Whatever it takes to make me walk again, I will do. How soon can we get started?" She was happy to have been given a sliver of hope to hang onto, however slim.

"Now that you are ready, we can start tomorrow. Sometimes an attitude adjustment is called for before physical therapy can truly be effective." The doctor tapped her on the leg. "In due time, I expect you to feel this. In the meantime, I have a fine young lady who will be here in the morning. She will explain what you can expect will happen during your therapy. She is going to work you until you will absolutely detest her, but keep the final goal in mind and try not to give in to the urge to strangle her, and believe me when I say there will be times you will want to."

"Surely she can't be that bad." Chris was puzzled. "After all she will be here to help me, won't she?"

"Just remember what I told you." The doctor gave her a wink before he turned to leave.

"Thank you, Doctor Gerard, for everything."

"Believe me, my dear, it's been my pleasure. Now you just hang in there, and we'll finish the job of getting you back on your feet. Then I expect you and your beau here to take me out to dinner." With that he slipped out the door.

"I'm sorry." She ducked her head, embarrassed to face Cam, who had been sitting quietly while the doctor was tending to her. "I guess he got the wrong idea about us."

"Don't apologize. It was a natural assumption, seeing how much time I have spent here in the last couple of weeks."

"I'm truly sorry. I can't seem to do anything but cause you and your family trouble."

She looked for tissue to wipe away the tears forming in her eyes. Before she found one, a gentle hand dabbed her cheeks before the tears soaked into her remaining bandages.

"See, I can't even cry without your help!" The more he wiped, the harder she cried.

"Please don't cry. It'll be all right, I promise." He had never felt so helpless in his life.

She tried to stop, but it was useless. Then, to her horror, she began to hiccup, loudly!

Ramona paused quietly just inside the door for a moment, watching the two of them as Cam tried clumsily to minister to Chris.

"My goodness, what's wrong?" She quickly approached the bed. "I thought everything was going pretty well." She took the box of tissues from Cam as he gave her a look of pure despair.

"Cam, why don't you go and get me a cup of coffee. I'll just sit here for a little while."

"Now tell me what's really bothering you," she asked Chris as soon Cam was gone.

"It seems that all I've done since Cam first came into my life, is to cause your family trouble. I'm so sorry," she finally got the words out between hiccups.

"I don't think I'd go so far as saying you have caused us nothing but trouble. It seems to me we have gained a lot from knowing you and your family," Ramona answered thoughtfully.

"How can you say that? Every time I turn around you are helping me out of some kind of trouble and now, here I am, in trouble again!"

"Now listen to me for a moment, and I will tell you who I think has helped whom."

She decided Chris needed a pep talk.

"I didn't realize just how useless my life had become since my Phillip's death. My time was spent tending my roses and living in the past, and then the twins came into my house and into my life. They made me look forward to getting up in the morning. They filled my house with laughter again, and soon I found myself joining in on their laughter. They have literally given my life back to me."

"You have enabled Robert and Kathleen to take a giant step forward with their business. I know for a fact they couldn't have left their children without you being there to take over in their absence."

"I'm afraid, my dear, you are very much mistaken if you think that you have given us nothing but trouble. Granted, you have given us some some worrisome moments, but I thank God every day for allowing you to come in our lives. Now dry those tears and concentrate on getting well. Do you hear me?"

"Thank you, Ramona. You can always make me feel better." She blinked away the last of her tears and gave the older woman a watery smile.

"Nonsense! I only spoke the truth because in the long run, I find that truth is always your friend."

"Here's your coffee, and I got some juice for you, Chris." Cam tentatively reentered the room, noting the tears were almost gone.

"Thank you, son," Ramona took her coffee and left him to help Chris with her juice.

"I thought this might make you feel a little better." He smiled uncertainly at her as he retrieved a small sack tucked under his arm and removed a small stuffed kitten with tag hanging around its neck. She couldn't resist a smile when she saw the name on the tag, "Chris".

"It's my very own kitten. I love it. Thank you." She hugged the toy tightly with her good arm. It seemed, no matter how bad she felt, he always knew what to do to cheer her up.

"The children would love to see you," Ramona told her. "How would it be if I brought them by tomorrow?"

"I want to see them too, but I'm afraid my bandages will frighten them." So far, she had only talked to them on the phone and had put them off when they asked to see her.

"I've explained to them that you have to stay in bed for a while, and you looked kind of like a mummy. They asked what a mummy was, so I showed them a picture of one. They want to see you anyway,"

Ramona explained. "It will do them both a world of good to see you. Especially, Jenny."

"If you think it best, I would love to see them."

"Is Celia still watching them?"

"No. There was an illness in the family, so she had to return home last week. Luci has been looking after them since then."

"All of them?" Chris tried to mask her surprise.

"Yes. She has been getting along very well with them," Ramona concealed a smile because she knew what Chris was thinking about Luci and children in general.

At first, Luci objected strongly to being put in charge of the four youngsters, but Cam had made it very clear to her that if she refused he would put her, Jon, and Jenny on the first plane home to Florida. He had been bluffing, but she didn't know that for sure, so she accepted responsibility for all of the children. Cam also informed her there would be no complaining to Chris about anything. So she hadn't mentioned it during any of her rare visits to the hospital.

The door opened quietly, and the children stood just inside the door, looking apprehensively at the room's occupant.

"Come over here, you two. I want a big hug from both of you." Chris stretched her good arm out to them. Cam gently nudged the youngsters nearer to the bed. He picked Jon up and sat him on the edge of the bed so Chris could reach him. "How are you doing, kiddo?" she asked the suddenly shy little boy.

"Is that really you?" he asked, trying to see her face.

"Yes, it's really me."

"Why are you all wrapped up?" he asked as he inspected the bandages.

"I had an accident. The car I was riding in went off the road, and I got some bumps and bruises so they had to wrap me up for a while. It's kind of like that time you scraped your knee and we had to bandage it, only I need a lot more bandages."

"Oh."

"Let's scoot down so Jenny can sit up there too." Cam helped Jon make room for Jenny.

"Hi, sugar." Chris hugged her little sister tightly as soon as she could reach her.

"Do you hurt?" Jenny asked as she carefully touched the bandages.

"A little sometimes, but I'm getting better every day," Chris answered her honestly.

"Why is your arm wrapped up like that?"

"It got broken in the accident, so the doctors had to put a cast on it so it would heal straight," she explained.

"Is it going to get well?"

"Oh yes, as soon as it heals, this cast will come off, and it will be as good as new." Chris squeezed Jenny again.

"Then I will be able to give you a big hug with both arms."

"Do they make you stay in bed all the time?" Jon asked.

"Yes, I have to right now, but soon I will be able to get up every day and exercise."

"Why do you have to do that?" Jon asked.

"Well, my legs don't work like they should, so I will have to have someone help me learn to walk again."

"You mean, you forgot how to walk?" Jon giggled at the thought of that.

"Well not exactly." Even Chris smiled at Jon's expression. "I know how to walk. It's just that my legs are weak, and I need someone to help me make them strong enough to hold me up again."

"Will that take very long?" Jenny asked as she settled back against Chris. It felt good to be leaning on her big sister again.

"I don't know. It could take a while, I guess." Chris wasn't quite sure how to answer that question.

"I was a little afraid that I wouldn't see you again." Jenny felt secure enough now to voice her fears.

"You've been talking to me every day on the phone. Didn't that make you feel better?" She pulled the little girl closer to her.

"Mommy and Daddy went away, and I remember talking to them on the phone, but they didn't come back. Jon and I talked about it, and he was a little worried too."

"Do you feel better now?" Chris asked the both of them.

"I sure do," Jenny answered, relief evident in her voice.

"I do too! But I wasn't as worried as she was," Jon bragged, but he was all smiles as he denied his concern.

"I think we had better go, kids," Cam broke in. "We don't want to wear Chris out."

"I don't want to go. I'm going to stay right here with Chris," Jenny scooted back tightly against Chris.

"Chris has to rest a while now so she can get her strength back and come home," Ramona explained to the determined little girl. "If you like, we can come back tomorrow. Would that be okay?"

"I think you should be able to come back every day from now on," Cam tried to help.

"If you will promise that we can come back tomorrow, I guess it will be okay," Jenny answered after she thought about it. "Do you promise we can come back tomorrow, and you will be here?" She turned to Chris for confirmation.

"Yes, sweetie. I will be here. I wish you could stay with me, but we have to follow the hospital rules." She gave each of them one more hug before she let Cam take them off the bed.

"Thank you for bringing them, Ramona." She caught the older lady before she left. "I sure have missed those two."

"I think it will do them a world of good. I suspect they will both sleep better now," Ramona replied.

"Have they been having trouble sleeping?"

"Well, not really. Jon has been very restless, and lately Jenny has begun having nightmares," Ramona reluctantly admitted.

"Why didn't you tell me?"

"I didn't want to worry you. Besides, Jenny settles right down when I put her in bed with me."

"Ramona, you shouldn't have to do that!" Chris exclaimed.

"I know I don't have to, but actually I sort of enjoy it. Kathleen had bad dreams when she was about that age. I did the same thing to soothe her. I figured if it worked for her, then it probably would work for Jenny because kids haven't changed that much over the years," Ramona reassured her.

"What about Jon? You said he had been restless?"

"I found that little boys are different. There would be none of that 'girl stuff' for him. So I just read the boys a story after they are in bed. Jon says he can sleep better if I leave a light on, so between the story and the night-light he seems to drop off fairly quickly."

"I'm sorry you have to go to so much trouble for the children," Chris apologized.

"It's really no trouble." Ramona grinned and added, "Actually, lately I have wound up with two little girls in bed with me on more than one occasion. I guess Sarah gets lonesome and she comes looking for company and I wake up with a little visitor on each side."

"Luci should be doing that." Chris made a mental note to speak to Luci about that the next time she had a chance to talk with her. It was bad enough that she had disrupted their plans, let alone their having to care for the twins when Luci was right there.

"How are you getting along with the children, Luci?" Her chance came later that evening when Luci stopped by for a quick visit.

"We're managing," Luci answered.

"How have they been sleeping?"

"Okay, I guess. I see that they have their baths and are in bed early every night."

"What do you do after you put them to bed?"

"Sometimes I go for a ride with Scott. He gets restless once in a while, and a drive helps calm him down," she answered, wondering where the questions were leading.

"Be careful with Scott. His driving put me here. I don't want you to end up like this or worse," she couldn't help but caution Luci.

"He drives okay. Maybe the accident put the fear in him." She laughed lightly.

"Nevertheless, be careful," Chris admonished her and then continued on the subject of the children.

"I wanted to talk to you about Jon and Jenny. Ramona tells me they haven't been sleeping well."

"I haven't heard any complaints from them." She bristled.

"No, because Ramona has been looking after them."

"Nobody told me anything about it. They have to tell me about things if they want me to know. What have they been doing anyway?" Luci tried to defend herself.

"Apparently Jon had been having trouble going to sleep, so Ramona has been reading to him until he gets drowsy and taking Jenny to bed with her when she wakes up with bad dreams. That seems to happen most every night."

"I didn't know that." Luci shrugged. "She seems to like the kids, so maybe she enjoys it."

"Regardless, Luci, the children are your responsibility. You should be watching them more closely," Chris chastised her older sister.

"I have to watch the kids all day. All four of them. I deserve a little break once in a while," Luci complained. "When are you coming home?"

"I don't have any idea. I expect it will be a while. In the meantime the twins are your responsibility twenty-four hours a day," Chris reminded her. "We have caused that family enough trouble without their having to care for two extra kids!"

"I'll try to watch them closer." Luci sighed. "Now, I have to go. Scott's waiting for me downstairs." Luci got up preparing to make her escape before Chris thought up something else to get on her case. "He said to say hello."

"Why didn't he come up?" Chris asked.

"He said he couldn't bear to see you like this. It makes him feel bad. Maybe when you are better . . ."

"I'll see you in a few days." With a wave of her hand, Luci fled the room.

Luci's answer confirmed her suspicion that Scott didn't want to see her because of her injuries. She accepted that because she knew that was what Scott was all about, just as she knew that her injuries had not been a factor in Cam's attention. Like it or not, he had become her anchor. It was his hand that gave her solace during those fearful times when she didn't know if she would ever see again. He was the one she wanted there when she was so terrified as they removed her eye bandages. If worse came to worse, she knew she would have had a strong shoulder to cry on without feeling like a fool; and if a miracle had happened and she could see, she had wanted him there to share in her victory.

Chapter Ten

"Hi. I'm Peggy Compton. I'm going to be your physical therapist. Dr. Gerard says you will soon be ready to go to work."

Chris was surprised at the girl standing at the side of her bed. She looked sort of like a pixie with her short red hair, freckles, and an infectious grin that seemed to run from ear to ear. That girl just couldn't be a physical therapist. Surely you had to be more than sixteen to do that!

"I'm sorry, I didn't mean to stare," Chris finally found her tongue. "But you are so young. Are you sure you know what you are supposed to do? Oh, I am sorry again," Chris apologized when she realized how rude she sounded. "I really didn't mean to say that. It just sort of popped out! Of course you are qualified, or you wouldn't be here."

"Please, could we start again?" A thoroughly embarrassed Chris begged.

"No apology necessary. I didn't hear a thing." Peggy didn't blink an eye as she moved up to the side of the bed to take the hand of her new charge.

"Hi. My name is Peggy. May I call you Chris?"

"Hello, Peggy, I've been looking forward to meeting you. I promise to try to keep my mouth under control from now on. Please, do call me Chris."

"I expect we will be spending a lot of time together, so let's not make any promises we may not be able to keep. Also, for the record, I hate looking like a teenager. Most people react just as you did. Fortunately, I have a good sense of humor, or you could be in serious trouble when I start working on you." She gently jabbed Chris's shoulder in an effort to put her at ease.

"Never the less, there is no excuse for the way I behaved." She was feeling less uncomfortable by the minute.

"It's forgotten. Now let's get on with the reason I'm here." Peggy opened a notepad she had in her hand and prepared to take notes. "Before we start anything, it will help if I know a little about you," she said as she slid a chair closer to the bed and sat down.

For a few minutes, Peggy asked questions about Chris and her family.

"Please don't think I'm being nosy when I ask you personal questions. It sometimes helps me if I know a little about the patient's mental state and how their mind works," Peggy explained the reason for her questions. "It sounds like you have both feet on the ground, figuratively speaking, so I expect only good things from you in the future."

"How soon can we get started? I want those 'good things' to begin as soon as possible," Chris asked as her hopes soared with Peggy's words.

"Let's not get too carried away." Peggy was glad to see eagerness in her charges eyes, but she didn't want her to expect too much all at once. "Unfortunately, things don't work quite that fast. We will have to start slow because of your arm. While it's in a cast, we are limited as to what we do."

"Can you explain the process of getting me to walk again?"

"To start with, I'm going to give you two deep leg massages a day, and you will spend some time in a whirlpool bath a couple of times a day," Peggy explained the first segment of her therapy.

"The nurses are already massaging my legs twice a day, and it hasn't done a thing for me." A glimmer of disappointment shot through her. "How do you think it will be any better if you do it?"

"All the nurses are doing is attempting to keep the blood circulating to prevent bed sores. Wait until you have one of my massages. You will definitely be able to tell the difference. I work on the muscles and nerves. The whirlpool will encourage blood flow and muscle tone."

"How soon will I know if I can walk?" She had to ask the question.

"Like I said, we will have to wait on your arm before we can try your legs, but a few weeks should give us a pretty good indication as to what is going on. Right now, patience is the key word."

"I've never felt that I have a great deal of patience, but I will do my best to take it one day at a time."

"Good." Peggy was satisfied for the time being. She was sure Chris would do her best, and that was all she ever asked of her patients. She genuinely liked the girl, and that was always a plus in her line of work.

"Are you busy?" Cam stuck his head in the door.

"No, we are just getting acquainted, and it's time for me to be moving on." Peggy stood to greet the new comer.

"Cam, this is Peggy Compton. She's going to be my physical therapist."

"Hi. I've seen you here before. I imagine our paths will cross again because I expect to be around quite often." Peggy extended her arm as Cam approached her.

"Peggy, meet Cam Eastland, my—ah—friend."

"Hello, Miss Compton. I'm happy to see you here. That means Chris will have to quit lying around in that bed and go to work for a change." He grinned at Peggy and winked at Chris as he took Peggy's extended hand.

"It's Peggy, please, and I promise to do my best to see that she earns her keep from now on."

"All right, you two." For some reason, her spirits soared as Peggy and Cam teased her.

"I'll see you later this afternoon." Peggy gave Chris a wave as she left.

"Cam, I'm glad you are here before the others arrive. There is something I wanted to discuss with you." She wasn't quite sure how to begin, but it was a subject that had to be brought out in the open.

"Then you had better tell me about it," Cam said as he made himself comfortable in a chair near the bed.

"This physical therapy. It's going to be expensive, isn't it?"

"Yes, I expect it will be."

"I've been worrying about that."

"The therapy?" He misunderstood what she was talking about.

"No, the expense. I've only just begun to repay you for the last time I was in the hospital. I won't be able to take care of Bobby and Sarah anymore. So that means I will have no income, and here I am running up all these new bills." There! She had voiced her concern. She waited for his reaction.

"Your medical bills here are being taken care of—" Cam started to explain.

"No, Cam. I can't allow you to keep paying my debts. There has to be another way! There just has to!" She didn't want to start crying again, but tears were forming in her eyes despite her best efforts to stop them.

"If you will give me a chance to explain." Cam stopped her. He didn't want tears any more than she did.

"You see, the accident was the fault of Scott. He is liable for all of your medical bills. His insurance company will pick up the tab for most of your expenses, and what is not covered is Scott's responsibility. Please believe me, when I say you will owe nothing to anyone as a result of Scott's screw-up."

"Is that really true? I don't have to worry about what all this is costing?" She couldn't believe her ears.

"Absolutely! I'm so sorry I didn't mention it to you earlier, but I honestly thought you knew about the insurance," he apologized, relieved to see the tears disappearing.

"All I want you to worry about from now on is getting well. Okay?"

"I'll try my best." Chris felt as if a great weight had been lifted off her.

"Did Miss Compton—Peggy explain exactly how this therapy is going to work?" He thought it was time to change the subject.

"Well, we can't do very much while my arm is still in the cast, but for right now she is going to do some kind of deep massage on my legs and have me take whirlpool baths twice a day. She says she wants to keep my joints mobile and get my muscles built up as much as possible. She says it will help when I go to work on the bars. I don't know exactly what they are, but I guess I will find out in due time." Chris was also glad for the new subject.

"It sounds like you soon will be on your way," Cam added, happy for Chris.

"I have to admit it will be nice to get out of bed for a little while each day."

"I was talking to Dr. Gerard the other day. He said that maybe when your therapy gets well under way, you can leave the hospital." Cam hadn't mentioned it until he had time to check everything out to be sure it could be arranged.

"Do you really think I can? It would be nice to leave here, but where would I go?" she asked, trying not to get her hopes up too much.

"To Robert's."

"But the therapy? I'll have to have it every day. I can't ask someone to drive me back here all the time. It's too far." She knew it was too good to be true.

"I've done some checking, and I found a way for it to work, if you're interested." Cam waited for her reaction.

"If I'm interested? You have to be kidding! Of course, I'm interested! Tell me what you found out." Her hopes soared once again. Maybe she could leave the hospital!

"Dr. Gerard gave me a list of equipment you will need, and he put me in touch with a gym equipment supplier. He promised to pull some strings and get everything we need. He will even deliver and set it up when it's time. How is that?" he asked, smugly.

"That's great! It just might work, except for one very important thing."

"What thing?" He thought he had covered all the bases.

"My therapy. Who's going to help me with that?"

"All taken care of. Dr. Gerard gave me the name of a nurse therapist. She will come live at the house for as long as we need her. All I have to do is call her. Peggy will come once a week to check on your progress," Cam replied. "Any more questions?"

"Just one. What in the world would I do if you weren't here to pick me up every time I fall?" Oh how she wished she could just give him a great big hug.

"There's nothing special about me, I can assure you." Cam smiled, a little embarrassed at the turn the conversation had taken. "If memory serves me right, this last time you didn't fall. My illustrious step brother knocked you down. I merely stepped in to offer my services. It's nothing that any self-respecting Sir Galahad wouldn't have done." He attempted to inject some humor into the suddenly serious conversation.

"I just want you to know how very much I appreciate what you and your family have done for me and my family. I'm not sure I could have survived this ordeal without you by my side holding my hand. Thank you," Chris tried to express her true feelings.

"Hi, Chris! We're here!" Jon's voice interrupted their conversation, much to Cam's relief.

"Come on in, kids." Cam lifted them to sit on the bed beside Chris and then moved to a seat across the room so Ramona could sit near Chris. "Okay, you two, let me hug you." Chris tried to move over to give them more room.

"How are you getting along with Luci?"

"She's okay," Jon replied after a moment.

"Don't tell her, but we like you better," Jenny leaned close to her ear and whispered.

"She's not as much fun as you are," Jon confided. "But she hasn't had as much practice as you have. I guess she has to learn how to play."

"I'm sure she's trying," Chris consoled them, secretly pleased that they preferred her over Luci.

"What have you been doing?" Chris asked.

"Mr. Sloane took us on a wagon ride once," Jon answered, "We went swimming three times and have picnics in the back yard once in a while."

"Mrs. Sloane lets us help her out in the kitchen sometimes," Jenny added. "Yesterday we helped her ice a cake."

"Don't get in her way," she cautioned. "What do you do with Luci?"

"Most of the time we go out into the backyard after breakfast for a while and play games," Jon replied.

"After lunch, we play in our rooms so Luci can take a nap."

"After supper we usually go out on the terrace with Bobby and Sarah's parents until bedtime," Jenny filled in the rest of their day.

"How did you sleep last night?" she had to ask.

"I went right to sleep and didn't wake up, even once," Jenny answered first.

"I didn't wake up either," Jon added.

"I guess I will have to get used to sleeping without the girls," Ramona spoke up. "That visit yesterday seemed to cure everyone's problems. The boys said they didn't need a story and wanted me to turn out their night-light."

"I'm glad. I hope they continue to sleep well. Maybe I should have let them come in sooner, but I had no idea they were having problems at night," Chris talked to Ramona while the kids were inspecting her cast.

"I guess we should have told you, but we were coping, and I didn't want you to worry. Besides, it's over now, and I don't expect we will have any more problems now that they can see you often. All we want you to do now is concentrate on getting well enough to come home."

"She starts her therapy this afternoon, so hopefully that won't be very far in the future," Cam joined the conversation.

"That's wonderful," Ramona exclaimed.

"Can we stay and watch?" Jon overheard what Cam said.

"Watch what?" Chris asked.

"What you are going to do this afternoon," Jon answered.

"My therapy? I don't think they will let you do that," she replied. "I'll tell you all about it tomorrow. Will that be okay?"

"I guess so," Jon answered dejectedly.

"Dr. Gerard tells me it's time for another session of plastic surgery. He wants to do it tomorrow, so I won't be here most of the morning. Maybe you should wait until after lunch to come back."

"Would you like some company while you wait?" Ramona asked.

"No, I will be fine," Chris assured her. "Thank you for offering though."

"I'll be here all morning," Cam spoke up.

"You don't need to, Cam. Really, I will be just fine. I'm sure you can find better things to do with your time than sit here and wait with me."

"I'll be here," Cam's voice told her there would be no arguing.

"How would you, kids, like some ice cream before we head home?" Cam lifted them off the bed in preparation of leaving.

"Yeah, I want chocolate!" Jon jumped at the chance of an icy treat.

Jenny was torn between Chris and ice cream. She edged back against the bed while she thought about it.

"Can we come back and eat it here and bring some for Chris?" She really wanted the ice cream; and if they came back, maybe she could stay a little longer.

"That's okay, sweetie, I'm going to have some for lunch. You go on and have yours with Jon." Chris understood her reluctance and encouraged her to leave.

"Can I see you tomorrow?"

"Of course you may. Now scoot!"

"I think it's almost lunchtime. How would you, children, like something to eat before we have the ice cream?" Ramona interjected, looking at her watch.

"Come to think about it, I am starting to get hungry. I didn't realize it was so late."

Cam told Chris he would see her the next morning and then led the twins out of the room while Ramona said her good-byes.

"Don't worry about the children, my dear. I'm quite sure they will get along just fine from now on."

"It's not in my nature not to worry about them, but as long as you are nearby, I don't worry quite so much. You have no idea how much I appreciate you."

"Jon and Jenny are a joy to have around. I'm just glad to be where I'm needed."

She patted Chris on the shoulder and bent to give her a kiss on the cheek.

"I guess I had better get out there before those three decide they will starve to death if they have to wait any longer on me. We will see you tomorrow afternoon if you feel up to it." Ramona took her leave just as they brought the lunch tray to Chris.

True to his word, Cam arrived early the next morning.

"Wake up, sleepyhead."

His voice roused her from sleep. She wasn't allowed breakfast, so to pass the time she decided to read, but after a few pages she nodded off.

"What time is it?" She blinked her eyes, trying to gather her thoughts.

"A little after eight."

"They were supposed to come get me at eight."

"I know. I was afraid I wouldn't get here in time to see you before you left." He grinned wryly. "I'm afraid I overslept. I stopped by the nurses station to see if you had gone, and they told me there had been a slight delay, so it would be about another twenty minutes before they were ready for you."

"Oh." Suddenly she couldn't think of any thing to say.

"Did they tell you how long this thing will take?" he asked.

"Dr. Gerard said he couldn't tell me how long it would take. I'll probably have to have at least three more operations. I didn't ask how long between sessions. Every time I ask someone how long anything will take, they tell me to be patient, so I guess I will quit asking." She laughed self-consciously.

"No, I meant this morning."

"Oh, sorry. I don't know. This is one of those times I didn't ask. I figure I'm not going anywhere, so it really doesn't matter how long it takes."

"I suppose you are right for the time being, but hopefully, it won't be too long before we can change that." Cam cleared his throat, having run out of conversation, himself.

For the first time since she had met him, Chris felt uncomfortable in his company.

Judging from the way he was fidgeting, she thought he probably felt he same way.

The next ten minutes passed with extreme slowness and absolute silence, each sneaking an occasional glance at the other, only to look quickly away when their eyes met.

"I'll go see what's keeping them." He jumped to his feet and made his escape.

"Please do." She was too slow with her request, and it was given to a closed door, for he was already gone.

"They are ready for you now." Cam reentered the room with two green-garbed orderlies and a gurney to move her to surgery.

Some time later, she didn't know how long, she roused from her post-surgery sleep to find Cam standing by her bed holding her hand. It felt so natural that all the discomfort she had felt earlier was gone.

"Hi, sleepyhead. I thought you were going to sleep all day." He quickly released her hand and moved to the foot of her bed as he teased her.

"What time is it?" she asked as she felt her new bandages. She had asked for a mirror earlier, but the nurse explained Dr. Gerard had ordered all mirrors be removed from her room until further notice. So she could only guess how she looked.

She knew that part of her head had been shaved, but as near as she could tell, the bare parts were covered with bandages. Dr. Gerard assured her that she would have a new crop of hair by the time the bandages came off for good.

"It's a little after one. The kids were here a little while ago. We didn't want to wake you, so Luci took them to a little park across the street. They should be back pretty soon."

"Could you roll the head of my bed up a little? I want to try to get my hair combed a little before they get here."

"It's too late for that. I see a pair of eyes peeking at us through a crack in the door." Cam opened the door wide enough to allow the visitors in.

"Hi, Chris, we were here a while ago, but you were still asleep, so Luci took us out to play for a while," Jon greeted her.

"Hello, kids. It's good to see you, Luci. I'm glad you came."

"Hi, Sis. How are you feeling?"

"I'm having trouble waking up for some reason or another, but I guess I'm fine," Chris answered as Cam raised the head of her bed.

"Luci, maybe you can help Chris comb her hair," he suggested.

"I think there's a comb in the drawer, Luci, if you don't mind. I could use a little help. It's awkward for me to do it with only one hand."

"Sure, I can do that." Luci found the comb and began running it through what part of Chris's hair she could reach.

"I'll sure be glad when I can wash it again. The nurses have used dry shampoo on it a time or two, but it isn't the same without water."

"Your bandages are different." Jon had been inspecting her face while Luci was combing.

"Yes, the doctor gave me some new ones this morning."

"Why?"

"Well, every so often they have to be changed, and this was the day for it."

"When will you get to take them all off?" Jon asked.

"I don't know. I expect it will be a while."

"Will you look different?" Jenny asked.

"It really doesn't matter what she looks like, Jenny. It's still going to be Chris." Cam cut in before Chris could come up with an answer.

"I don't care what she looks like. I just want her to come home," Jenny said a little sadly.

"I want you to come home too." Jon didn't want to be left out of the conversation. "I don't care what you look like either."

"I will be home just as soon as the doctors will let me because I miss you two little monkeys too," Chris tried to lighten the conversation.

"The doctors haven't given you even a hint as to when you can leave here?" Luci asked as she replaced the comb in the drawer and turned back to Chris.

"Don't have any idea, but I hope it won't be too much longer, now that I am starting therapy on my legs."

"I certainly hope it will be soon. The kids need you there." Luci glanced quickly at Cam as she spoke.

"Mr. Sloane took us out to see a brand new baby horse this morning," Jenny told Chris.

"It's not a baby horse, Jen. It's a baby colt," Jon corrected his sister.

"Okay. Baby colt. It sure is cute. It has white feet and a white stripe on its face."

"What color is it?" Chris was glad to change the subject.

"It was all black, except for the white on it. Mr. Sloane said they are going to name it Midnight Storm because it was storming when it got here last midnight," Jon answered.

"Did it rain last night? I thought I heard thunder once, but I didn't hear any rain," Chris asked.

"We had some rain and a little thunder, but it was nothing serious," Cam replied. "It seems to do a lot of that sort of thing over here."

"I kind of remember Kathleen saying something about a lot of dampness here, on the way from the airport. It seems like a long time ago," Chris spoke quietly. A little sad at the thought of having been in England all this time and, except for that first day, all she had seen was the inside of this hospital.

"Have you been back to that little pub we all went to?" She didn't want to dwell on sadness, so she changed the subject.

"You mean the one where we got slaughtered at darts?" Cam took the hint. "No, not yet. But when we do go back, you can bet we won't be throwing darts with the locals."

"Well, it certainly didn't take those men long to send you all back. Kathleen said it had to have been the shortest game on record." Chris grinned at Cam, glad to tease him for a change.

"We'll all go there again before we go back to Florida," Cam added. "I'm thinking about asking them for some lessons."

"It sounds like lessons might be a very good idea," Chris commented solemnly.

"Thanks. I really needed to hear that. You may have totally wrecked my dart throwing ego." Cam feigned anger.

"Sorry," Chris answered straight faced.

"You don't sound very sorry," Cam retorted.

"Chris?" Jenny patted her on the arm to get her attention.

"Did you get your ice cream yesterday?"

"Yes, I did. It was strawberry."

"That's the same kind I had. Was yours good?"

"It sure was."

"I had chocolate," Jon joined in on the conversation.

"I guess it's about time to leave, kids." Luci had stayed as long as she could stand it. She had "borrowed" some money from Chris's purse, when no one was looking, and she wanted to do a little shopping before they returned to Kathleen's and the other children.

"It's time for all of us to go." Cam noticed Chris smother a yawn for the second time. "I think it's time for Chris to take another nap."

The door had barely closed before she dropped off for the nap Cam had predicted she needed.

"Are you awake?" This time it was Peggy who roused her from sleep.

"Hi, Peggy. Is it time for another massage?" Chris shook the last of the grogginess out of her head, anxious to continue the process of seeing if she could walk again.

"Yes, it's time for you to get back to work."

Peggy had been right when she told Chris she would be able to tell the difference between the nurse's gentle rubbing and her massages. But after two weeks of pummeling, massaging, and whirlpool baths, she could feel no changes in her body. On the verge of giving up, she decided to have a serious discussion with Dr. Gerard and Peggy the next day. She intended to try to pry an honest opinion from each of them as to her chances of ever having the use of her legs again. If they agreed with her, and she was terrified they would, she would ask Cam to get her a wheelchair and take her back to Florida so she could get on with her life. She would do her best to accept the situation as gracefully as she could.

Something, she didn't know what, roused her from a sound sleep that night. She lay for a moment, listening. Then she felt it. A tickling sensation running from her ankle up the calf of her leg. Absently, she reached down to rub it when suddenly she remembered. Her leg! She felt something!

Before she could decide what to do, a pain the likes of which she had never experienced knotted her calf. She barely had the strength to call for the nurse when she collapsed against her pillow as a second pain tied the arch of her foot in a knot.

As soon as the nurse saw Chris, she followed the instructions Peggy had left earlier, and within minutes Peggy arrived on the scene.

"Which leg is it?" was all she asked before setting about massaging the knots away.

"What is happening to me?" Chris asked as soon as she was able to talk.

"I think we are about to witness the beginning of another real life miracle." Peggy had seen this happen many times before, and each time she felt overwhelmed by it.

"What do you mean?"

"Every time I begin therapy on someone, I pray that I can be of some help. I never know how long it will take to get to this point, or if it will get there at all. When it does happen, I invariably feel blessed to have had even a small part of helping someone to walk again."

"Are you telling me I will walk again?" Chris felt a rush of excitement shoot through her.

"When I first looked at your x-rays and tests, I gave you a fifty-fifty chance of mobility."

"After our first interview, I upped the odds to sixty-forty because I heard the determination in your voice and saw the near panic in your eyes at the thought of never being able to walk again and take care of your brother and sister. Well, kiddo, if we can get the other leg to kick in like this one did tonight, I would say we have upped the odds considerably."

Before they could talk any longer, another round of muscle cramps started. The difference with these was that Chris didn't mind the pain at all.

"Can you explain to me what is happening?" Chris asked when the pain subsided for a few minutes.

"Well, in layman's terms. The massage and whirlpool therapy is designed to help keep your muscles pliable. Eventually, we hope they will get tired of just doing what I tell them to do and rebel. That's great because it means they will begin to listen to you and do what you tell them to do, instead of doing what I make them do. I would say that if you try really hard, your big toe just might move a little for us right now." Peggy pulled the sheet back so they could both see her feet. "Now I'm going to run my fingernail up the bottom of your foot. Tell me if you feel anything."

"I felt it. It tickled!" Chris laughed out loud. "I can actually feel something down there!"

"Now comes the biggy. Try to wiggle your big toe." Peggy was afraid to breathe until she saw it move.

"I'm trying but it won't do anything. Oh look! It moved! It actually moved! I can't believe it!" Chris looked at Peggy. "Did you see it?"

"I saw it. You did it!" Peggy let her breath out.

Then both girls burst into tears.

"What's wrong? Should I call Dr. Gerard?" Miss Brenner, the night head nurse, entered the room to find both occupants with tears streaming down their faces.

"We don't need a doctor." Peggy was the first to recover. "Nothing is wrong. In fact, we are doing quite well."

"Then why the tears?" a very confused nurse asked.

"Pure joy, Miss Brenner. Pure unadulterated joy," Peggy answered, and then she turned to Chris. "How would you like to drink a toast to that wiggling toe?"

"I would love one."

"Miss Brenner, would you bring us two orange juices and one for yourself if you have the time? I think a little celebration is on order."

As they were waiting for the orange juice, Peggy turned to Chris. "Now you have to remember that the other leg has to kick in before it is truly a victory."

"Is there a chance that it might not come around?" She hadn't even thought of that.

"I have heard of cases where that happened, but only rarely and not once in any case I've been involved in."

"How long do you think I will have to wait before we know what's going to happen with me?" Chris landed back in reality with a thud.

"In previous cases, I've seen the time vary from a few hours to a few weeks. No two are alike. I think I will make arrangements to stay here for a few nights so I will be nearby when it happens."

"When it happens. I sure like the sound of that." Chris felt a little more hopeful about her future than she had since the accident. "One more thing. Could we keep this quiet until we know more? I don't want to get everyone's hopes up in case nothing happens."

"What do you mean, in case nothing happens?" Peggy stood with hands on hips and glared in mock anger at Chris.

"Well, you know what I mean," Chris stammered, not quite sure if Peggy was really upset with her or merely teasing. "It will be a bigger surprise if both legs have feeling, won't it?"

"I guess as long as we know what is happening, it's not necessary for anyone else to know about it. So, for now, I'll keep your secret," Peggy agreed to the request.

"I just hope it will happen soon." Chris fervently hoped she didn't have to wait too long.

Peggy was there, almost immediately, as Chris got her wish two nights later. She learned what the phrase "grin and bear it" truly meant that night. Peggy assured her that every pain was a step forward in her ultimate goal, so she accepted the suffering for what it would give her in the end.

The crisis had passed by the daylight hour. Having kept a close eye on them during the night, Miss Brenner brought in three glasses of orange juice when they were ready to mark the second milestone.

"Has the doctor said when your cast will come off?" Peggy asked as she relaxed a few minutes before leaving.

"I think he's planning to remove it sometime next week."

"Good. I'll get you fitted with a brace to strap on your arm, until your arm muscles regain their strength. Well, I'm off. I'll see you in a couple of hours. You had a rough night, so I will take it a little bit easy on your morning workout, but look out for the afternoon one! Now try to take a nap if you can. Dr. Peggy's orders!"

"It's time for me to make rounds, so I will leave you also. It might not be a bad idea if you did try to get some sleep." With that admonishment, Peggy and Miss Brenner left Chris alone to rest.

She tried to settle for a nap, but her mind wouldn't let her sleep. She wanted Cam to get there so she could tell him about her progress.

"What happened?" Cam asked as soon as he saw her face.

"What do you mean?" She hoped no one had told him.

"You look different. Your eyes are sparkling, and if your grin gets any broader, I swear you face will split. Are you going to tell me, or do I have to go ask your doctor?" he threatened.

"How about I show you? Pull the sheet off my feet."

"I've seen your feet before. Tell me."

"Come on be a sport," she pleaded.

"Now what?" He pulled the sheet back and looked at her feet.

"Look at my toes." She concentrated on moving her toes as she had been practicing for the last few hours.

"Chris! How long have you been able to do this? How much can you feel? Why didn't you tell me?" He could think of a hundred more questions, but all he really wanted to do was kiss her, which he did, much to her surprise and his.

"Cam!" She had hoped to surprise him, but he turned the tables on her. His kiss had released a myriad of feelings within her. She certainly liked it, but that wasn't good because it was probably spur of the moment and wouldn't be repeated. On the other hand, what if he really did like her? No, he was out of her reach. She wasn't nearly sophisticated enough for him, and besides she had to think about Jon and Jenny.

"I admire you so much, Chris. You've survived all of this because you are a fighter. I knew you could do this! I just knew it!" The kiss had a very unsettling effect on him also. He had to keep talking because he was afraid his emotions would overwhelm him if he stopped. "You have come so far. I always knew you could do anything when you set your mind to, and now you have proved it!"

"Peggy says, I can start to try my legs out next week, just as soon as I get this cast removed. I can hardly wait. She says I have a very good chance of walking again, but that I shouldn't get too anxious because it will take a lot of hard work. She's going to have me fitted with a brace for my arm to use until it gets its strength back." Once she started talking she couldn't seem to quit. "I feel I'm finally making some progress. A few days ago I was ready to give up, and then this happened, so now I feel like I have a new lease on life!"

"Whoa, slow down and tell me exactly what happened."

She explained the events of the last few nights to Cam, making light of the intense pain she had endured and dwelling on the first movement of her toes, laughing and demonstrating it over and over again just because she could.

Chris repeated her good news to Ramona and Kathleen as soon as they arrived, bringing more tears and hugs all around.

"Did Peggy tell you how long it will take before you will get all your feeling back in your legs?" Kathleen asked.

"No, she says it's only a matter of time before the surface nerves start reacting to touch, but it will probably be a while before the muscles and deep nerves begin to respond. She says I have a long way to go, but that's okay because I'm on my way and nothing can stop me now." Her exuberance was contagious, and soon there wasn't a doubt in the room as to her full recovery.

The surface feeling had mostly returned to her legs, but despite her best efforts, she was yet to move anything but her toes. There was no doubt in her mind that as soon as she stood, her legs would somehow remember what to do. So it was with full confidence that she would have some measure of immediate success when she faced her first day of trying to stand.

Peggy made one last check to be sure the braces were properly in place and fastened securely on her arm and her legs, then rolled her chair to the end of the exercising bar and locked the wheels of the chair firmly in place.

"Now place your hands on the bars in front of you, and we will help you stand," Peggy explained what was going to happen. She had asked another therapist to assist her.

"Carol, if you will take that arm, I will stay on this side. And when we are ready, I will give the word and we will all go at once."

"Okay, let's get you to your feet."

Chris held on as tight as she could, but if it hadn't been for Peggy and Carol, she would have collapsed in a heap on the floor. Much to her horror there had been absolutely no reaction from her legs. They may as well have been rubber for all the use they were!

"Don't worry," Peggy told her as they sat her back down in her chair. "A lot of the time we don't get it right on the first effort. In a minute we will try again."

The second try was no more successful than the first. After a third attempt, Chris collapsed in tears, and she hadn't been able to stop.

"Please stop crying." Peggy felt so helpless. She had tried to warn Chris about expecting too much with her first attempt at standing. "This is not helping anything, besides you are going to make yourself sick."

Peggy knew from experience that it was better to let the disappointed girl get it of her system now than give her a sedative to calm her down, but that didn't make it any easier for her to stand by and watch.

"I'm trying to, but you don't understand. Nothing happened when I tried to stand. Nothing! They should have at least held me up! I didn't expect to walk, but I should have been able to stand!" Chris got that out between her sobs.

"Please listen to me, Chris," Peggy pleaded with her. "So we didn't do so hot the first time. That doesn't mean that we just give up! I've told you all along it would take time, patience, and a lot of hard work if we are going to be successful."

"All the hard work in the world won't make my legs work if they are dead! That's what they feel like! Dead! Even the braces didn't help!" Chris took a deep breath and finished what she had to say. "I may as well quit wasting your time. When Cam comes in I'll ask him to get me a wheelchair and take me home."

"I would never have taken you for a quitter." Peggy prayed that Chris would have enough pride to take exception to her words. "Had I known that you would give up the first time the going got tough, I would never have taken you on as a client! I don't waste my time on quitters." With those words, she wheeled and walked to the door, pausing before she left to add one more barb. "Evidently you don't think as much of your little brother and sister as I gave you credit for." With that she quietly closed the door behind her, leaving the orderly to take Chris back to her room.

Chris lay for some time in a state of shock. She replayed Peggy's words over and over in her mind. Never in her life had she been called a quitter nor had her feelings for Jon and Jenny ever been brought into question.

Somehow, she managed to get through the evening without breaking down in front of her visitors. Kathleen and Ramona had voiced concerns about her. Neither of them believed her when she assured them she was just fine but chose, for the time being, not to pursue it. Cam knew something terrible had happened. The question was *what*.

He remained seated after the others had left, looking intently at her pale face and swollen eyes. He had hoped that she might tell him if they were alone.

"What happened, Chris?" he asked, finally. He was guessing it had something to do with her therapy but he needed for her to tell him about it.

"Nothing! I'm just fine. Maybe a little tired from sitting up today. A nurse took me on a tour of the hospital, and I guess it took more out of me than I thought." Luckily, she hadn't told anyone that she was going to try to stand today. She couldn't face any questions about that right now. She had intended to ask Cam to take her home; but something, maybe her pride, prevented her from doing so.

"Is there anything I can do for you? Anything at all?" he tried again.

"No! I mean I'm just fine. All I need is a good night's rest. Don't worry about me. I'll be all right. I'm a survivor!"

"If you ever need anything at all, please call me." He knew he would get nothing more here tonight, so he decided to talk to Dr.

Gerard and Peggy as soon as he could. Maybe they would fill him in. "If you ever need a shoulder to lean on, Chris, I hope you know that mine is just a phone call away." He stood, for a moment waiting for a response from her. When there was none, he took her hand and bent over to tenderly kiss her forehead.

"If you are sure there is nothing I can do to help, I'll leave you for tonight and see you in the morning. Sleep well." After one more concerned look at her, he quietly left the room.

It took every ounce of resolve she had to hold the tears at bay until Cam was out of sight, but the second the door closed behind him, they fell like rain.

"May I come in?" Peggy cautiously stuck her head into the room the next morning, unsure of her welcome. She knew from talking to the nurses that Chris hadn't made any arrangements to leave the hospital, so she took that as a good sign.

"Of course." Chris managed a wan smile. She had been trying unsuccessfully to eat breakfast. She wasn't sure it would stay down even if she were able to swallow it.

"Chris, I am truly sorry for my outburst yesterday. I should have realized how deeply disappointed you were," Peggy apologized.

"Apology accepted." Chris took the hand offered by Peggy. "I acted like a fool. I should be apologizing to you."

"You have nothing to be sorry about. It was a normal reaction. I should have handled it better."

"The truth is, that outburst of yours is probably the only reason I'm still here. I couldn't sleep last night, so I did a lot of thinking. At first, I resented being called a quitter, but later I came to the conclusion that I would be just that if I left the hospital," Chris admitted. "I also came to a second conclusion, which involves you. At least, if you will stick with me for a while, it will."

"I will do anything I can to help you. I hope you know that." Peggy was relieved to hear those words from Chris.

"First I want your honest, and I do mean honest, opinion as to my chances of ever having use of my legs again."

After a long moment, Peggy answered. "There is never a guarantee in cases like yours. However, it is my gut feeling that with a lot of hard work, you can be one of the lucky ones. That's about the best I can do."

"That's all I wanted to hear. That I have a chance." Chris breathed a sigh of relief. "If you will help me, I will try to do anything you ask of me, and more. I will try never to have a meltdown again. I have to walk again. I just have to."

"You don't know how happy it makes me to hear you say that." Peggy could have hugged her. "Since you have had such a rough night, I think it might be better if we wait a day or two before we try again."

"Can't we do it today? Really, I feel fine."

"No, you need to be fully rested. Besides, I want to take some more measurements and bring a different type of leg brace for you to try. It will take a day or two to get them ready," Peggy explained why she wanted to wait.

"Do you think the new braces will be better?"

"They will give you total support at first, and then as you get stronger we can back them off as we need to. I should have used them first, but I honestly thought these would work. It was a mistake on my part, and I do apologize for that. I'm sorry I didn't explain what I was trying to do, so maybe we could have avoided last night. I didn't get much sleep either, so you didn't exactly suffer alone."

"I do feel a little washed out," she admitted. "So I guess I wouldn't mind having an easy day. I'll start by having a nap as soon as I finish my breakfast." Chris suddenly felt very hungry.

"You don't get the whole day off because we still have massages and whirlpool, so I will be back in a couple of hours." Peggy turned to leave with an admonishment. "Eat up. Take my word for it. You will need your strength for what I have planned for you. See you later."

She had barely finished breakfast when Cam arrived, determined to find out what was troubling Chris, one way or the other. He had planned to go to the job site with Robert, but first he had to see if he could help Chris. If need be, he was prepared to stay at the hospital all day if that's what it took to find out what was upsetting her.

"How are you this morning?" he asked, noting her empty breakfast tray.

"Much better now that I've eaten," she answered as she pushed her tray away. "It's amazing what a good night's sleep will do for a body."

"Are you sure?" The dark circles under her eyes belied her words; however, she did sound a little brighter. "You seemed so down last night that we all were worried about you."

"I don't need anyone worrying about me. I do have a right to be a little down once in a while, don't I?" Chris answered tersely.

"Of course, you do. It's just that you've never shown that side of you," Cam tried to explain what he meant.

"Well, now you know my little secret. I do have my moments. Are you disappointed in me?" she asked. Trying to put up a good front in order to get Cam to quit asking questions.

"Quite the contrary, it's nice to finally find out that you have your flaws just like all of us other mortals." A slightly relieved Cam took a seat near her bed. Maybe things weren't as bad as he feared. At least she had some of that fire back in her eyes.

"Isn't it a little late for breakfast?" He thought it was time to change the subject.

"Breakfast was on time, I was late eating because Peggy stopped by for a few minutes," she answered, relieved to talk about something else. "Are the children coming in today?"

"I don't know, I guess so. I thought I might go to the job site with Robert in a bit, but I will call Ramona to tell her you want to see them." He was supposed to call her anyway to tell her what he found out about Chris.

"Am I in time for breakfast?" Robert stuck his head in the door.

"Hello, Robert, I'm sorry but I emptied the tray. Come in. It's nice to see you again."

Chris was relieved to have someone interrupt the conversation before Cam could ask any more questions.

"How are you doing today?" he asked as he moved closer to the bed to look at Chris.

"All things considered, not too bad. I'm a little tired this morning, but I'm going to remedy that with a nap before Peggy gets here." She hoped her explanation would satisfy them so they would quit asking how she was and leave her alone. She needed time to reassess her future. She had an idea that it was going to require a lot more work than she could possibly imagine if she were to walk again.

"I'm about ready to leave, Cam. If you want to go with me, we had better shove off." Robert was anxious to get to his job site. Chris sounded much better than he expected, so he thought Cam would probably go with him instead of staying there to talk to the doctor and Peggy.

"I'm ready, but first I need a minute to call Ramona," Cam answered Robert then turned back to Chris. "I'll tell her to bring the kids. Do you need anything? Maybe a book or something?"

"A book would be nice. Ask her to pick one for me. I think that's all. Thanks."

"Well, we're off. I'll see you this evening." Cam moved to the door.

"Take care, Chris. I'll see you soon," Robert bid her good-bye as he followed Cam out the door.

An hour's nap did wonders for Chris. By the time, Peggy returned she was awake and feeling much better.

As they talked while Peggy massaged, her resolve was strengthened, and she once again felt the she had a future that didn't include a wheelchair.

Two days later, she was once again in the training room. This time—with Carol on one side and Peggy on the other, and a brand new set of braces on her legs—she managed to stand, not by herself, but that didn't matter. The accomplishment exhilarated her, so she was more than a little disappointed that Peggy refused to allow her to try to take a step.

"But, Peggy! I know I can do more!" She objected as they helped her to return to her chair. She stood up two more times. Then Peggy called a halt for the day.

"Not on the schedule, I'm afraid." Peggy turned a deaf ear to her plea. "Remember, we talked about this. First we stand a while, then we move on." Peggy wasn't about to do anything to cause a setback.

Within a week, Chris took her first step. Granted, she had a lot of help, but it sure felt good to go through the motions anyway.

How she wished Cam was there so she could tell him, but he was on another short trip back to Florida. She felt guilty for keeping him from his work. She tried once halfheartedly to convince him that he didn't need to stay there for her, but thankfully, he told her things were going quite well with Peter in charge. He kept on top of things by the telephone, and only occasional visits were needed to handle a few things personally.

Everyone else was thrilled with her news. Robert sneaked a bottle of champagne in for them to celebrate the occasion. Kathleen just "happened" to have paper cups in her purse. They all got caught by the floor nurse, who promised not to tell on them if they gave her a sip. That's all she could have, but she wanted that taste! The only one missing the celebration was Cam.

Later in the evening, he called to see how her day had gone and to wish her a good night. When she told him about the step she had taken and the champagne, he insisted on sharing a belated toast with her. She asked the nurse to bring her a glass of orange juice while he searched for something to drink with her.

By the end of the next week, Chris was actually taking a series of steps with the aid of Peggy and the exercise bars. Peggy agreed it was time for Chris to leave the hospital, but she could only go if Peggy were allowed to oversee the installation of the exercise equipment and have a role in planning her long-term therapy.

Chris quickly agreed to that, partly because she respected Peggy's ability as a therapist, but mostly because she genuinely liked the girl and was reluctant to lose her as a friend.

Cam immediately put the wheels in motion to have the equipment installed at Robert's house and made arrangements to have the two therapists meet to discuss Chris's long-term therapy.

Chapter Eleven

It was with a great deal of anticipation and a certain amount of sadness that Chris prepared to leave the hospital. She had formed friendships with much of the staff, many of whom had stopped by to wish her well. Some of them even got together and bought her a new gown and robe set to wear home because they teased her that she had worn all of the old ones out.

Three days later, Cam and Ramona transported their precious cargo home on one of the few bright sunny days they had seen since being there.

Chris leaned back in her seat and drank in the lush scenery all around her. It was more magnificent than she remembered. For the first time she truly felt as though she was actually making some headway towards getting some of her old life back.

Ramona had explained to the children what to expect when Chris arrived home, so they were not unduly upset to see her in a wheelchair. Most of the bandages had been removed from her face, exposing a number of her scars. They were curious about them, so Chris encouraged them to touch her face while she explained that when the time was right, the doctors would make most, if not all, of them disappear.

The scars and wheelchair were soon forgotten as the children began telling her about the party they were going to have that evening. But first, Cam told them, she had to rest for a while. He carried her upstairs to her room. The lift over the bed intimidated her when she first saw it; but when he explained its function, she decided it might have potential.

"Now, I will leave you to Luci so she can get you settled for a nap. I will see you later."

"What do you want me to do?" Luci was at a complete loss as to how to cope with an invalid.

"Well, first I guess I need to get this robe off and then get under the covers," Chris suggested.

When she awoke, she found four pairs of eyes peering at her from the foot of the bed.

"Hello. What are you all doing down there?" she asked.

"Looking at you," Jon answered.

"Why?" She was amused at their expressions.

"Waiting for you to wake up," Jenny responded. "Cam said we couldn't wake you up, but he didn't say we couldn't watch you until you woke up by yourself."

"We are ready for the party, but we can't start until you are there. Are you going to be ready soon?" Jon wanted to know.

"I'm awake, so I guess I will be ready soon." Chris grinned, relieved that things were getting back to normal for the children. "Can one of you go get Luci for me?"

Jenny went in search of Luci while the rest of the children went downstairs to tell everyone that Chris was awake and would soon be ready to come downstairs.

When Chris was ready, Cam picked her up and carried her to the top of the stairs.

"I'll show you the new toy I had installed for you if you are ready for it." He placed her in a chair attached to a rail on the side of the staircase.

"Now, when this bar is in place across your lap, you just have to push this button, and you get a free ride to the bottom. How is that for convenience?" he asked her.

"I don't know. Are you sure it's safe? Those stairs look awfully steep."

"It's absolutely safe. If you want I'll hold your hand the first time down."

"I would be glad for the company. Are you sure it won't go too fast?" she asked doubtfully.

"It will only go one speed: slow. I promise."

"If you say so. Get ready because I'm going to push the button." She might as well get it over with. Gingerly she pushed the button, squeezed Cam's hand, and closed her eyes as the chair began the descent to the bottom of the long staircase.

"You can turn loose now," Cam reminded her at the bottom of the stairs as she sat there frozen even after they stopped.

"That wasn't so bad, was it?" he asked.

"It wasn't as scary as I expected," she admitted.

After a few minutes of discomfort, Chris joined in on the gaiety of the party. She felt like they were genuinely happy to have her there. After an initial greeting, Scott did his best to avoid looking at her, and as soon as he was finished eating, he excused himself, pleading a headache.

Everyone, including Chris, knew why he left; but no one mentioned it, choosing instead to continue with the festivities for a little while longer.

After the meal, Mr. and Mrs. Sloane entertained the group with traditional songs of Ireland and England. After a few songs, they invited the others to join in, so the evening quickly turned into a happy songfest.

"Luci, I think it's time to take Chris upstairs. We can't wear her out the first night here."

Cam suggested. Earlier, he had asked Luci to take over the personal needs of her sister.

Luci had given up her pursuit of Cam after he explained to her, in no uncertain terms, that there was not now or would there ever be anything between them. He threatened again to send her, Jon, and Jenny back to Florida if she continued her pursuit of him. As before, he was bluffing, but she couldn't take the chance that he was. Since then, she had been a little intimidated by him, so she was reluctant to refuse anything he asked of her even though she would rather have had someone other than herself care for Chris.

"It's been a long day for you, Sis. It probably is a good idea if you are ready," Luci agreed with Cam.

"I guess I am a little tired. It's been so nice this evening, being here with all of you. You have no idea how much I appreciate everything you've all done to make me feel so welcome." Chris paused to thank everyone.

"Of course, you are welcome here," Kathleen spoke for everyone. "We are just so glad that you are well enough to be here with us, and you are welcome for as long as you wish."

The trip upstairs was much more pleasant than the previous one down the stairs, so Chris decided she might even be able to overcome her fear of it in time.

"Good night, little one. Sleep well, and I will see you in the morning," Cam murmured as he carefully laid her on the bed.

The bed felt so good to Chris when she finally got settled in for the night. Luci did her best, but she definitely fell short in the nursing department.

Susan Hayes arrived early the next day. Peggy had introduced the two of them the previous morning when the two therapists got together in Chris's room to discuss her home therapy.

Susan was altogether different from Peggy. She had a quiet efficiency about her as opposed to Peggy's bubbly personality. They were, as Chris soon discovered, equally good at their job.

Much to Luci's relief, Susan took over the complete care of Chris. She taught her how to move from the wheel chair to another chair or to bed without great difficulty.

Cam provided another wheelchair for her downstairs so she would have the convenience of one on each floor.

The chairlift no longer frightened her so she used it often.

During the days that followed, Ramona spent time with Chris every day. She talked about her past, her family, and how she came to wed Cam's father.

"Phillip and Justin had been best friends, just as Margaret and I were. Justin and I first met at Phillip and Margaret's wedding. We were married nine months later."

"Margaret died a short time after Cam's birth. Phillip was so devastated that he just couldn't cope with a new baby, so he asked me to care for him for a little while. He finally got his life back together and took Cam to live with him after almost a year."

Ramona smiled, a little sadly, thinking about that time. "How I missed that little boy."

"It must have been terrible for you," Chris sympathized with her.

"Justin and I had been married for nearly nine years when he was killed in a construction accident. Kathleen was five and Scott was two. Phillip took care of everything for me during that awful time. He planned the funeral, fed the kids, made me eat, and helped me cope with all that had to be done."

"I moved back with my parents afterwards. Phillip and I didn't see each other for eleven years. We exchanged cards and children's pictures at Christmas, but that was the extent of our contact."

"We met, quite by accident, at a party given by mutual friends. After that time, we discovered that we still had a great deal in common. So much that we were married three months later. I'll never know if we married out of love or friendship, but either way, I was extremely happy, and I have no doubt that Phillip felt the same way."

"Not too many people get a second chance for that kind of happiness, even if only for a little while," Chris reminded her when she paused, lost in thought.

"How old were your children?" she asked.

"Cam was twenty and a fine young man. A little too serious, but a real asset to his father. He was away at college, so we didn't get to see him all that often."

"Kathleen was seventeen, and Scott was fourteen. They both resented Phillip at first. It took a lot of perseverance on his part, but he finally won Kathleen over. It took almost a year, but one day she decided she adored him. The final straw came when she liked this young man, and I strongly disapproved of him. Phillip persuaded me to allow her to go to a school dance with him, and the rest is history."

"I don't think I understand," a curious Chris asked.

"I doubt that I will ever live that down." Ramona smiled. "That young man whom I disliked so is now my son-in-law."

"I guess everyone is allowed to be wrong once in a while," Chris chuckled with Ramona.

"It was different with Scott. He never really accepted Phillip's authority. He was always very good at covering his feelings. So good that even now I'm never sure what he is thinking. But one thing I do know is that he is not the man I would have liked for him to have become." Ramona paused, and then finished quietly, "He can't face you, you know. Because of what he did to you. He wants to go home. Cam offered him a job at the factory, but he says that if he can't go back to the top, he won't go at all."

"I worry because I don't know what will become of him. I can't—won't support him forever. Sooner or later he's going to have to grow up and make his own way."

"Maybe, when we get back to Florida he will settle down." Privately she had her doubts about that happening, but she tried to comfort Ramona.

Chris could feel herself improving with the dawning of each new day. Just being out of the hospital helped her mental state. One morning, she even caught herself humming along with a song on the radio. It was then she decided that in or out of a wheelchair, it was great to be alive.

Two

Then one day Scott and Luci disappeared. Chris wondered where they got the money until she looked in her purse. Then she knew where some of it came from because all the money she had brought with her plus the month's salary Robert had given her was gone.

"Where could they have gone?" Chris wondered aloud, near tears that Luci would stoop so low as to steal from her sister.

"I want to know where they got the money," Cam wondered.

"I'm afraid I know where they got some of it," Chris admitted. "All the money in my purse is gone."

Cam was absolutely livid when he found out about the missing money. Not because they were gone, but because they had upset Chris.

Chris was more than a little frightened at what Cam might do when he found them. Fortunately for Chris, she had little time to worry about Luci because the next day she returned to the hospital for an overnight stay for her next round of plastic surgery and an evaluation by Peggy on her progress.

"I admire you so, Chris," Cam told her as they waited in her room for the doctor to see her before she left the hospital the next morning.

"How can that be? I can't walk, I'm all scarred up, and I have been nothing but a financial burden since we met," she asked. "If only I had listened to you that night and not gone with Scott, none of this would have happened. Then you could spend your money where it's needed, on the factory and helping other people." She burst into tears.

Cam dropped to his knees in front of Chris and held her tightly in his arms, letting her cry out some of her frustrations on his shoulder. When her tears stopped, he took out his handkerchief and began gently wiping them away.

"Aren't you afraid that saltwater from your tears will burn your face?" he asked as he continued to dab at her face, or what he could of it.

"You always have worried too much about me." She gave him a watery smile. "Now you are worrying about my scars. Most people would want me to cover them up, and here you are wiping them off."

"I'm not most people." He tapped her on the nose. "Keep that in mind in the future."

"Thank heaven for that." Feeling much better, Chris straightened up and began trying to smooth her hair.

"You are progressing very well," Dr. Gerard pronounced as he examined her before he dismissed her. "I believe your plastic surgeries are coming along very nicely, and when they are finished, I don't think there will be anything left to remind you of your injuries."

"Thanks for the words of encouragement, Dr. Gerard, but right now I am more concerned about my physical abilities than how I will look. Do you have an opinion about that?" Chris asked.

"I've talked with both Peggy and Susan, and I've looked at all your tests results. Your muscles seem to be filling out nicely, so I see no reason not to expect a full recovery, provided you keep up the hard work. I gather from Susan that hard work is not a problem for you." The gentle man patted her shoulder as he answered her question.

"No, it's not a problem." Chris smiled as the Doctor rose to take his leave. She felt great relief at his prediction.

Chapter Twelve

Chris returned home and quickly settled back into her daily therapy routine.

A week passed before she heard from Luci. Then she got a phone call from her.

"Luci! Where are you?" she demanded as soon as she recognized her sister's voice.

"I'm in Paris. Please don't be mad at me, Sis," Luci pleaded with her. "Scott told me he had some contacts here. They were hiring models, and he promised to get me a job if I would come with him. I didn't know about the jewelry, honest I didn't. He told me about it after he had pawned it in London and we were on the plane."

"What jewelry?" Cam's voice thundered in their ears.

"Cam! Have you been listening in on our conversation?" Chris was as surprised as Luci.

"I'm sorry, Cam. I don't know where he got it. He just showed me the money he got for it." Luci's voice wavered in fear of Cam's anger.

"Where is he?" Cam's voice was stone cold when he asked the question.

"I don't know where he is. He spent most of the money we had, and then took off with the rest of it. That's why I'm calling. I can stay here for one more day, and then I have to leave. I don't have any money or anywhere to go." How she wished she were only talking to Chris. She knew her sister would bail her out, but Cam was in charge now. "Please let me come back, Chris. I promise to do anything you ask of me."

"You know I don't have any money to send you. You already took it all." Chris swallowed her pride and turned to Cam. "Cam, I hate to ask you, but could you help me out again?"

"No, I don't think you should come back here, Luci."

"Cam!" She couldn't believe her ears.

"I'll tell you what I will do, though," Cam continued. "I will loan you enough money to get you back to Florida and to last you for sixty days. At the end of that time you are on your own, and I expect to be paid back within one year. Do you understand what I am telling you?" Cam wanted to be absolutely sure she was clear on his offer.

"I don't know, Cam. Can't I come back there so we can talk it over?" Luci stalled for time.

"That's the offer, Luci. Take it or leave it. There is nothing to discuss," Cam spelled it out for her. "And there will be no running to Chris every time you get in a bind. Is that clear?"

"Chris?" She appealed to Chris.

"Sorry, Luci. It sounds like a more-than-fair offer to me," Chris fully agreed with Cam. "If I were you I would take it and be grateful."

"How soon can you send the money?" Luci gave in for the time being because she was sure she could change Chris's mind when she got to talk to her in private.

"I'm leaving very shortly for London. I'll wire the money to the United States Embassy there. I would advise you to be on the next plane to Florida and not to waste any of the money on any pipe dream you may still have."

"Listen to him, Luci. Be careful and call me when you get home," Chris bid her sister good-bye.

"All right, Sis. Good-bye."

"Ramona, would you like to tell me about the missing jewelry?" Cam asked her shortly after hanging up the phone.

"How did you find out about it?" she asked.

"Luci told me that Scott pawned some, so I knew it had to come from you. How many pieces did you give him?"

"I didn't give them to him," she admitted reluctantly. "I didn't tell you because I knew it would upset you."

"So it has come to that. He's so desperate to get away from here that he steals from his own mother." Cam sighed, feeling nothing but sadness for what Ramona must be going through. What was he going to do to try to make it right?

"I'm really sorry. I wish I could have prevented it from happening."

"Don't feel too badly for me. It's my own fault for bringing the jewelry with me. I should have left all of it at home," Ramona tried to make Cam feel better.

"What pieces did he take?"

"The ruby and diamond necklace and earring set your father gave me as a wedding gift. The diamond ring he gave me for our fifth anniversary and the pearl necklace and earring set that Justin gave me when we were married."

"I'm so sorry this happened." Cam couldn't have felt worse if it had been his own. "Well, I guess I had better get Luci's money sent to her before somebody throws her in jail or worse."

"Where do you suppose he is?" Ramona wondered.

"It would be my guess that he went back to Florida. We'll call Ellen in a day or two. I wouldn't worry too much about him. He's a big boy, and he can take care of himself if he has to." Cam hugged his stepmother. "I can't bear to see you unhappy, so I will do what I can to help him get on his feet."

"Thank you, Cam. It's nice to know that I have one son that I can count on." She hugged him back, feeling a little better about everything.

"You made my father very happy, and for that I will be eternally grateful, so I will do what I can to help you. I only wish it could be more."

"Now I think I'm going to cry."

"Hey! Let's not get maudlin." Cam laughed self-consciously, trying to avert tears if he could.

Cam enlisted Robert's help to comb all the pawnshops near the airport in London.

Four hours and a small fortune later, they had successfully retrieved all the pieces of jewelry.

"I thought I would never see them again," Ramona burst into tears the minute she saw her jewelry. "I promise this will never happen again because from now on, I will keep them under lock and key. How can I ever thank you both?"

"No thanks needed," Robert answered. "In fact, I rather enjoyed poking around those shops. I wouldn't mind doing that again sometime. How about you, Cam?"

"I hadn't thought about it, but it was an interesting way to spend the afternoon," Cam answered. "I wonder if Everett has any pawnshops."

"I don't know, but I think we ought to check it out," Robert answered. "There is no telling what we have missed out on."

※

A telephone call to Ellen confirmed Scott's whereabouts.

A few days later, Cam left for Florida intent on having a serious conversation with Scott about his past conduct and his future plans.

He found Scott lounging by the pool and not at all glad to see him.

"I think it's high time we had a talk, Scott." Cam came to a halt near where Scott sat.

"You can take a load off, if you want." Scott indicated a nearby chair. "But I don't know that there is anything for us to discuss."

"I think that might be one of the problems. You and I haven't talked as much as we should have." Cam hesitated, unsure how to start. "For as long as I can remember, I've had my life all planned. After college I went to work for my father, and then when the time was right, I was going to take over his businesses."

"Since I can remember, my father and I had only each other. Then, suddenly, there were three other people sharing my father's life," Cam continued thoughtfully. "Every time he came to see me at college, all he could talk about was how happy he was with Ramona and how proud he was of Kathleen and you. When I came home, there you all were taking up the time he normally spent with me. I deeply resented losing that time. I was so jealous of you all that I started looking for excuses to stay away. You were the reason I decided to start up my own company. Dad just couldn't wait to bring you into the business with him. He said he wanted us to work together. Well, maybe I had to share my father with you, but I wasn't about to share my work with you." Cam was talking more for his own benefit than Scott's right then. He had never put his feelings into words before.

"You have no idea how it felt, having the perfect son crammed down my throat every day!" Scott interjected angrily. "Why didn't I do well in school, like Cam? Why didn't I go to college, like Cam? Cam didn't have any trouble with the police when he was your age. Why are you? Cam had a job by now. Why aren't you working?"

"I didn't know about that. Maybe we have more in common than we think." Cam looked thoughtfully at Scott then continued, "I was amazed at how my company took off. I felt very smug that I could be so successful, independently of my father. Then, one day I found out that a great part of its success was due to his influence. He was persuading people to give me work. I was so angry with him for that. He let me blow off steam for a while, then he sat me down and explained a few facts of life to me. He may have had a hand in getting me the initial contacts, but it was strictly up to me to keep them. If I couldn't provide the service required to stay competitive, then no amount of his influence could help me. So in reality, I was on my own."

"I didn't completely forgive him." Cam hadn't thought about that in a long time. "But I think I understood why he did it."

"I was glad when I heard you were starting up your own business," Scott admitted. "I figured then the Eastland factory would be all mine to run. I had planned on having years to learn how to run it. It was a lot harder to be in control than I expected it would be."

"It's never easy to take over in the manner you were forced to." Cam thought he was beginning to understand how Scott must have felt. "That last weekend when Dad came to see me, he asked me to fly to Miami with him to look over a business he was thinking about investing in. We took that time to make our peace with each other. I was on my way home with Dad, to try to sort things out with your mother, Kathleen, and you when the plane went down."

"I discovered what a truly good person your mother is while I was in the hospital. Despite grieving for my father, she was there for my every need. She sat with me while I was in constant pain after I woke up from the coma. I honestly don't know if I would have lived if she hadn't been there to encourage me every step of the way." Cam explained his feelings for Ramona. "She was so proud of the way you took over at the plant that I decided maybe you weren't totally hopeless after all," Cam continued.

"I didn't know any different until the company lawyer called to explain the financial problems they were having. He told me that a great deal of money was missing, and they had traced it back to you. It seemed that you had been making large cash withdrawals without reporting it. He told me that you had left on vacation before it was discovered."

"I asked him what my options were. He said, if it were him, he would take bankruptcy and close the doors. I couldn't do that to my father's memory, so I did the next best thing. I invested some of my own capital and cut back substantially on the employees. I didn't feel up to the task, mentally or physically, of running the operation, so I brought in a good man, named Peter Kelso, to stabilize things. Pete tells me now that we're in the black, and he thinks we can start rehiring people very shortly."

"I'm glad," Scott confessed. "I really felt bad about all those people losing their jobs because of what I did."

"So now we come to you, Scott. What do we do about you? You've broken your mother's heart, and your sister is ready to wring your neck."

"I'm truly sorry for my actions," Scott apologized. "But how can I possibly undo all the damage I've done and start over?"

"First, I would call your mother and apologize. I think that's all she will ask of you. Incidentally, it might also save your scrawny little neck from Kathleen's hands."

"But what about the jewelry," Scott asked quietly. "How do I ever make that up to her?"

"Robert and I were able to track all the pieces down and return them to your mother." Cam related the fate of the jewelry. "I expect full repayment for all it cost us, by the way."

"I can't begin to tell you how much I appreciate your bailing me out of this mess." Scott shook his head in disbelief. "I thought I had blown it for sure, I can't believe you would do something like that for me."

"Actually, I did it for your mother. I'm not sure I would have done it just to save your sorry hide," Cam admitted candidly, feeling more ambivalent toward his stepbrother than before their conversation had begun.

"As I see it, Scott, you have two choices. You can continue the lifestyle you have been following. But if you do, you will no longer be welcome to live here, and you will have to support yourself. Then you will be able to do as you wish with your life."

"Or, you could be one of the new employees at Eastland. You will start at the bottom and learn the business from there up. You will draw the same salary as anyone else in your position," Cam spelled out the rules. "You gave up the right to any control of the business when you stole from it. If you keep your nose clean and prove you can be responsible, then when the time is right, I will be happy to give the business to you and Kathleen, if she wants it. If she's not interested, then it will become all yours because I want to return to my own company."

"I would suggest you think carefully before you give me your answer," Cam finished.

"I don't have to think about it, I know what I want to do," Scott answered after a short pause.

"While I was on the plane coming home, I had plenty of time to think. On the whole, I've had a pretty good life. The trouble was that I was so busy complaining about what I didn't have to realize that. I was too self-centered to even make an effort to try to understand what a fine man your father was. I've taken a long hard look at myself this last few days, and I don't much like what I've seen," Scott admitted quietly.

"I appreciate what you have done for all of us, and if you think I can make it, I would like to go to work for you. I will give my best effort on any job you see fit to give me. I also appreciate you're coming here and talking to me like this. I understand a lot of things now." Scott stood up to offer his hand to his stepbrother by way of an apology.

"I'm glad to hear that, Scott. I've no doubt that you can do anything you set your mind to and do it well." He stood and accepted his stepbrother's hand.

"Your mother will be so proud of what you are doing." Cam slapped Scott on the back.

"When Ellen told me that Luci was back, I went to see her," Scott continued. "In fact, I've seen her every day and we have had several serious conversations about our futures. She has given up any idea of becoming a model and wants to go to night school to prepare for a new career. She doesn't know what she wants to do just yet, but what she really needs right now is a job because she knows the free ride is over, and from now on she wants to pay for whatever she gets," Scott spoke up for Luci.

"You gave me a second chance, and I would really appreciate it if you could see your way to do the same for her and give her a job too." Scott held his breath waiting for a response.

"Will wonders never cease?" Cam didn't disappoint Scott. "If she truly wants a job, I see no reason why she can't have one there too. I will mention it to Pete so he can make it happen for both of you. Let me be very clear though, once you are on the payroll, there will be no favoritism. You both will either sink or swim on your own merit."

"Understood," Scott accepted the terms gratefully. "Now I am going to call Luci and give her the good news." He paused, then continued, "I've discovered that Luci and I have a lot in common, and I'm going to do my best to find more. In fact, I intend to court her, and if she will have me, I would like to make her my wife someday. When we are both adult enough to handle marriage, that is."

"Somehow, Scott, I think the two of you should get along very well." Cam was quite surprised at this turn of events. "The first time I laid eyes on Luci, I felt the two of you were well suited. Probably not for the same reasons I believe you are now, but nonetheless I still think you are a good match. And I, for one, hope that she will have you."

"I need to make a quick phone call before you get on the phone with Luci." Cam felt a sudden urge to talk to Chris. "I want to catch the next flight back to London. I think it's high time I did a little courting of my own."

"I assume you're talking about Chris," Scott guessed.

"That's right."

"That's funny. Even though I didn't like the idea, I knew she would be a better match for you than me. Maybe the only reason I wanted her was so I could beat you at something, just once." This time, Scott really didn't mind losing to Cam. "If we play our cards right, maybe we will both get lucky."

For the first time in their lives, the brothers shook hands, wished each other well, and truly meant it.

It was early afternoon before Cam arrived at Robert's. After greeting Ramona and the children, he went in search of Chris. He found her in her favorite spot, in front of the window in her room, enjoying the scenery.

"You are looking better all the time," Cam greeted Chris.

"Hi, Cam, I didn't hear you come in." Chris turned to face him.

"In fact, I didn't know you were back." She had been so lost in her thoughts that she failed to hear him enter the room.

"I just got back. I wanted to let you know that both Scott and Luci are safe and sound in Florida."

"I'm glad. You weren't too hard on them, were you?" she asked. She had been more than a little concerned about Cam's reaction upon seeing the both of them for the first time since they had disappeared.

"They're both still in one piece, if that's what you are asking." He smothered a smile when he saw her let out a sigh of relief.

"Surely you didn't think I would do bodily harm to them?" Cam laughed.

"No, not really," she admitted. "But the thought had crossed my mind that they both did deserve a good shaking for what they did."

"Enough of Luci and Scott. Pete tells me that the factory is doing very well. In fact, he says that very soon we can start rehiring some of the laid-off people."

"I wish I could be one of them." She sighed. "I'm going to need a job as soon as I'm well enough to go back to work."

"If you really want to go back to work there, I can personally guarantee you a job as soon as you are strong enough, if you still want it, that is."

He wanted to tell her how he felt about her, but the words wouldn't come. He had never done this sort of thing before, so he didn't have a clue how to begin.

"Thank you. That makes me feel better to know I have the promise of a job to look forward to. Even if I never get to go back to school, at least I'll have enough money to care for Jon and Jenny."

"Chris, I have been wanting to—" he began.

"Are you ready?" Susan stuck her head in the door. "Oops, I'm sorry. I didn't know you were back, Cam," she apologized for interrupting.

"It's okay. We were just talking." Cam started to leave when Chris stopped him.

"Cam, wait a minute. Ramona and Susan are going to help me try to walk today, without my crutches, I mean. Would you have the time to give me some moral support?"

"Just try to keep me away," Cam answered.

A few minutes later, with Ramona on one side and Susan on the other, Chris stood to face Cam. She kept her eyes on him as she handed her crutches away.

"Come to me, Chris." He held his arms open to her. "I'll catch you."

The only sound in the room was the scraping of a foot across the tiled floor. She took her first step, then a second, and a third.

"Come on, Chris, you can do it. Just put one foot in front of the other," Cam encouraged her when it appeared she would stop. "Just two more steps, and then you will be here in my arms where you belong."

Suddenly, she realized just how much she wanted that. All she ever wanted was to be in his arms. Just to have him hold her in his arms.

"Just one more step, Chris, just one more," Cam pleaded.

"Here I am. Catch me." She collapsed in his arms.

"I've got you." Cam enfolded her in his arms. Her being there felt so right. "I promised you I'd catch you, didn't I?"

"Yes, and I believed you. I haven't felt this safe since my parents died. I thought that feeling was gone forever. Thank you for returning it to me." She hugged him as if she would never let him go.

"Well, it's about time! I don't believe they need us right now." Ramona, very pleased with this turn of events, smiled at Susan as they both quietly left the room.

As soon as he realized they were alone, Cam swept her up in his arms and carried her to the nearest chair and nestled her on his lap, keeping his arms wrapped firmly around her frail body.

"I've wanted to do this for so long." Cam gently and thoroughly kissed her.

"That makes two of us that wanted that," Chris answered as soon as she regained her breath.

"I didn't know it, but I guess I fell in love with you the afternoon that I picked you up out of that ditch," Cam admitted. "I have to confess, that I found your purse before I left your house that first afternoon, but I wanted an excuse to return."

"I was glad to see you again."

"While I'm confessing, those sweaters you left in the car after the party, I hid them under the back seat so I would have another excuse to come back to see you."

"I would have been disappointed if you hadn't returned," she shyly admitted.

"I didn't plan on having you faint in my arms, but it worked out rather well. For me, I mean. I was sorry you were sick, but as least I got to keep you in my life a little longer."

"I don't know what I would have done if you hadn't been there," she admitted.

"I knew I should have told you who I really was, but I was afraid that if I did, you would walk out of my life, and I would never get the chance to know you," Cam tried to explain his actions.

"I thought I was beginning to get your attention when Scott came along and screwed up everything." Cam winced as he thought about how close he came to losing her. "I could have strangled him when I thought he was taking you away from me. Then along came Luci to really complicate things."

"When you had the accident, I thought I would go out of my mind. At first, I was terrified that I could lose you forever. And when we learned that you were going to live, but there was a chance you would never see or walk again, I wanted to beat Scott within an inch of his life with my bare hands. Then I blamed myself. If I hadn't come down so hard on him, maybe he wouldn't have been so upset. Maybe, I should have just insisted that you stay there and not go with Scott until he cooled off." Cam closed his eyes, trying to block out those memories.

"Now I feel as if we've been given a second chance at life, and I, for one, want to make the most of it. I love you, Christine Walker, with every fiber of my being." He sat frozen, waiting for her reaction.

"How can that be? You don't know if I will ever walk normally again. I have scars that might never go away." Oh how she wished with all her might that she could be the one for him, but she knew in her heart that wasn't possible.

"Chris, I am in love with you, and only you." Somehow he had to convince her. "I love your intelligence, your sense of humor, the way you laugh, even the way you cry. To me that's the whole person. When I look at you I don't see scars or braces. I see the woman I am hopelessly in love with. How she happens to be wrapped is of no importance to me." He held her close, praying she would believe him.

"Are you sure, Cam? Really sure?" She felt a glimmer of hope starting deep within herself.

"Please say you will marry me, my darling, because I don't think that I can survive without you by my side. I want to take care of you.

I want to grow old with you. I want to help you raise Jon and Jenny, and I want us to raise our children together, if that's what fate has in store for us."

"Oh, Cam. I do love you." She could hardly believe this was really happening. "I think I have loved you for a long time, I was just afraid to admit it, even to myself, because I didn't really believe this could happen. Of course, I will marry you."

"Do you believe it now?" Cam breathed a sigh of relief at her words. "How soon can we be married?" He didn't want to give her a chance to change her mind.

"I would marry you tomorrow, but I'm going to ask you to wait a while. I want to be able to walk down the aisle on my own two feet as the whole person you deserve."

"I doubt that I will ever deserve you, but as long as you promise that you will marry me, you can take all the time you need. And when you are ready, we will be married."

"Cam?"

"Yes?"

"You talk too much. Shut up and kiss me."

"With pleasure. This is going to be one of my favorite things—"

The End

About the Author

Joyce Armintrout was born in a farmhouse near Peculiar, Mo. She grew up in that same house and has definite country roots. By the fifth grade, she was writing short articles about things in her daily life. During her eight grade she became interested in Western action stories because she found out her father had been a real cowboy in his younger days. She made up tales about things that might have happened to him while he lived on the ranch in Wyoming.

Shortly after entering high school, she discover the romance novel, so her subject matter changed again. She turned to the teenage romances going on around her. Anytime there was a breakup, the couple involved were apt to be the subject of her next story. While she was employed at AT&T, she was often called upon to create crossword puzzles and other word games in conjunction with their safety programs. She also wrote short skits to be performed in front of the monthly safety meetings. She never outgrew her love for the romance novel. Her characters became more mature, with different problems. Her retirement gave her more time to pursue her writings. She divided her time with her short stories, memory pieces about her life growing up on the farm without electricity or running water, and her family history. Mostly her writing has been for her own enjoyment. This is her first attempt to become a published author.

CPSIA information can be obtained
at www.ICGtesting.com
Printed in the USA
FFOW02n1653140115
10187FF